PEARLS

MEL TAYLOR

This book is a work of fiction. Any reference to historical events, real people, or real places are used fictitiously. Other names, characters, places, and events are products of the author's imagination, and any resemblance to actual events or places or persons, living or dead, is entirely coincidental.

ISBN-13: 978-0692554951
ISBN-10: 0692554955

This book is dedicated to the memory of
Jean Perwin.
She was my lawyer. My advisor. My friend.

Chapter 1

Brent Solar chewed on crushed ice soaked with rum and coke, staring at the ultra tight skirts in the two bar stools nearby, smiling at both of them and wondering which one he would ask to the table.

One black. One blonde.

This was Brent's night. Everything was perfect. He tapped the briefcase with his foot, making sure the case was always near him. The blonde smiled at him one more time, letting her tongue glide over her lip, slow, seducing, eye-catching with an unspoken message meant only for Brent that sent blood rushing to areas somewhere below his belt.

The other one had brown skin smooth as poured syrup. She turned to Brent, with a split blouse open down to her waist, exposing rounded cleavage, making Brent's eyes widen.

A waiter walked past, and Brent made him lean down so he could whisper a directive. Brent pulled out a hundred from his roll and gave it to the waiter, who nodded and headed toward the bar. Two drinks were placed in front of the women, who raised their glasses and grinned a thank you to Brent Solar. He returned the smile, then checked his watch. 12:40a.m. The meeting was less than twelve hours away. The most important meeting in his life.

That was then.

Right now, the women needed to finish their drinks. There was still plenty of time. Brent tapped the briefcase one more time with his toe. Everything was perfect. Life was good.

Brent stopped chewing ice. The two women picked up their drinks and walked toward him. In watching their movements, Brent was lost in the sway of their hips, the way the fabric hugged their breasts and the incoming smells of perfume now enveloping him in a wafting, moving cloud of aroma and smiles.

"What's your name, Sweetheart?" the blonde said, sitting down.

"Brent."

"You got a last name, Brent?" the other one said, her ebony fingers wrapped around her drink.

"Solar. You know, like the sun." Brent laughed. The women did not, opting instead to stare at him.

"My guess was, you were someone special from out of town. You here on business Brent?" The blonde whispered the name Brent, the way he imagined he would hear it in the middle of a phone sex conversation.

"We've been watching you all night," the other one said. Her eyes were bright and brown with a dash of something sparkly on her eyelids.

"Yeah, we noticed you've been watching us since we first walked in." They both nodded in agreement and laughed.

"I'm sorry. I didn't mean to stare."

The blonde said, "That's okay sweetheart. We know you've got a big decision to make." She never stopped smiling as she moved her red-tipped fingers across the table until they rested on his hand.

"Decision to make?" Brent tried not to look too confused.

"A decision." The ebony fingers put down the drink. "You were trying to decide which one of us you would try and take back to your hotel room." She paused, then looked directly into Brent's eyes. "You want to get one of us into bed, don't you?"

"I,I," Brent tried to form words.

"Sure, sweetheart. It's tough we know. But I can make it very simple for you." She patted the top of his hand, sweeping her fingers over his drink hand making sure to touch his skin before bringing her manicured fingers up to her chin.

"You can?"

"Sure," the blonde said. "You can have both of us."

He felt the first kiss on the base of his right cheek, causing impulses to rocket through his body. Then a second kiss on his forehead. They were coming at him from both sides, rubbing soft hands all over, giving his senses a ride he never had before. The room was ahead of him. Brent needed some help from the two of them as they made it up the stairs to the second floor of a low-rent hotel on Federal Highway. He aimed the key card at the slot, leaned a shoulder on the door and led them inside the dirt-gray carpeted room with twin beds and the loud hum from a leaking air-conditioner.

"I don't know your names." Brent put the briefcase up on a chair.

"Oh, it's easy," the other one said. "We find it funny. We both have the same name."

"Sweetheart, we're both called Pearl." The blonde was staring at the beds. "Pick which one."

"Pearls?" Brent spoke the word to no one in particular. His head was a mass of dancing shadows, his thoughts like steel wool, no longer sharp in his movements, losing perspective on what was real and unreal. The Pearls were taking off his clothes, undoing buttons, removing his shoe and easing him back into bed. Brent heard the zipper move on his pants, then four hands easing off the rest of his clothes. Images started to blur.

The blonde leaned down to him until their lips met. A warm long kiss sending Brent into a deep comfort zone. This was his night. Everything was perfect.

With each kiss, he let go of all reservations. He just wanted to ride the emotions. Let it ride, let it ride.

Brent sensed he was on a carpet ride of hands easing him over the mountain tops, touching his chest, massaging his exposed legs, caressing his forehead and arms. The perfume was close to his face. She was now on top of him. He tried to wrap his arms around her.

"Ow, Sweetheart. Your watch is getting tangled in my hair."

Almost robot-like, Brent undid his watch, missed placing it on the table, and watched the timepiece drop to the carpet without making a sound.

"Lay back," black Pearl said from somewhere in the room, "We got it from here. You will feel like a new man."

He closed his eyes and let them take over. Brent wanted to stay awake but he could not. His body was in the midst of being touched all over. He felt himself drift into another world, dropping deeper and deeper, getting darker, until everything around him looked like a charcoal mist. He was hearing instructions and doing what he was told. Just do what they want.

Chapter 2

She only wore the scent of early morning sex. Brent kept repeating that one thought in his mind as he leaned into the pillow to smell the fragrance of the Pearls. A single shaft of sunlight touched his right eye and he peeked out at the morning. The room was dark. A row of shades was almost closed. Brent started to get up and fell backward with the pain of his headache. He crushed his eyelids shut as if that would ease the thunder in his head.

Thoughts of the night crept into his morning memory. He was wearing boxer shorts, no shirt and black sox. He looked across the room through rum-weary eyes. The closet door was open. He got to his feet, holding both sides of his head. The room swirled about him for a few minutes before he got his bearings.

Take stock. He did a survey of the room. The first thing he noticed was his suitcase was missing from the closet. The thought hit him like a ramrod. Brent looked down at himself and realized he was wearing the only clothes he had left. Pants, shirt, belt, all gone. He looked around for his cell phone. The phone was missing. Panic and anger swept through him.

Despite the cobwebs, Brent moved quickly about the room checking for his belongings. His thirty-five thousand dollar Rolex was missing. Now he remembered, there was four thousand dollars in his right pants pocket. Another ten-thousand was in the left pocket. All gone with the missing pants.

He snapped his head toward the floor safe. The door was open and the safe was empty. He had stuffed almost eight-hundred-thousand dollars in the safe. Fear now gripped him as he turned toward the chair where he placed his briefcase. He slammed open the door of the closet, checking the corners of the space. He checked the storage area above, moving the iron out of the way, jamming his fingers into the corners of the space looking for something that wasn't there. Brent pounded the right side of the closet. He stepped back. Reality set in.

The briefcase was gone.

"No!" Brent shouted, arms flailing at the air. "No, no, no." He reached for the room phone and called the service, jamming the phone against his ear. "What time is it?" he asked. "Eleven-thirty?" Brent was shouting again. He slammed the phone down.

The remaining clear cells in his brain were snap-firing thoughts on what he should do. "I'm dead," he said to himself. "Dead, dead, dead!"

He took the room in the low-rent section of town to avoid public contact. His money would be okay here. No one would think to find that much money in a low-rent motel safe. This was a place to hide.

He replayed the minutes from the early morning. "The Pearls," he shouted to the room. Through the hazy thoughts, he remembered how the blonde Pearl placed her hand over his drink. What did she put into his rum? A roofie, perhaps. "Think," he shouted to no one. "Think!" He looked down at his naked wrist, minus the watch. "Damnit," he shouted.

The meeting was less than thirty minutes away. The upfront money from the interested buyers was gone. All of it. Brent circled the room three times in his shorts trying to figure his next move. He called to room service again and explained his clothes somehow got wet. Five minutes later, a man delivered a change. Clothes left behind months ago from a guest. Now he could operate. Once dressed, he headed for his next stop.

The bar.

Brent Solar kept telling himself he was not a violent man. His specialty was computers, logistics and watching over documents. Everyone trusted him with secrets.

This was different. He was pissed. And scared. Damn scared. Three quick steps into the bar and the place looked different with a heavy fill of sunlight. The night bartender was gone, replaced by a new man. His face was turned away from Solar, bent over, placing glasses on a lower shelf. He had no warning as Solar clamped both hands together like a wedge then drove his hands into the man's neck, causing him to crumple to the large floor mat.

"I need the night man's name and address. And I need them now," Brent hissed. His words were fueled by his anger. A moment of silence only made Brent angrier as the man looked confused. When he didn't answer, Brent took his foot and stepped on the man's neck injury. That brought groans. Brent reached into his pocket and pretended to have a gun. The man on the ground raised both hands in a defensive mode. "This is the last time. What is the name and address of the night man?"

"Stan," the man said softly. "Stan Willows. Lives on Fifth next to the bridge. By Lexington."

Brent got the man to give him the exact number address. "Where's your cell phone?"

The man reached into his pocket, grimacing the entire time and produced the phone. Brent snatched it with his free hand, then stuffed the phone in his pocket. "Thanks. You're doing great. Just two things. First, have you heard of two girls, both calling themselves Pearl?"

The man shook his head, then backed up it up. "No. No Pearls."

"Good. And the second thing. If you try and contact Stan, I'm coming back here and rip out your heart. Is that clear?"

"Yes. Yes. I won't say anything. I promise."

Satisfied, Brent Solar backed out of the bar then turned into the bright south Florida morning and walked to the office where the good-natured motel clerk set him up with a car. Brent smiled.

Seconds after Brent left the bar, the dayside man rubbed his sore neck. Nearly a minute later he was able to sit up. He grabbed at his head as if the pain was taking over and moving down through his chest. As he sat on the ground, he didn't notice the two men who entered the bar.

From his sitting position on the ground, the man finally noticed the men and the guns aimed at him. They were longer than normal hand guns because of the suppressors attached. Investigators will tell you during a robbery the victim never notices the faces of the thugs, only the gun. The man on the floor was asked a question. "You have surveillance cameras here?"

The man nodded and nervously pointed to the two spots where they were placed. The taller man approached. "Tell us what you told him." The man on the floor repeated the address.

On this idyllic day, outside the bar, palm trees stood erect, fronds dipping only slightly, as the soft pounding of runners moving down the street added to the calm. Three irregular-shaped clouds held position against a sky, blue as waters of the Bahamas. Cars rolled by, joining the daily stack-up of traffic. No one would hear the quiet burps of five shots tearing into the head, chest and arms of a man sitting on a bar room floor.

Chapter 3

Black Pearl smiled. She rested flat on her back in the bed, covered neck to feet in money. "Pour some more on," she yelled across the room. "I want to feel every dollar on my body."

"You gonna stack that money back together? That's a lot of stuff." Blonde Pearl was at a desk examining the watch. "We can get some good money for this thing."

The woman on the bed tossed stacks of bills in the air, watching them intensely as the greenbacks floated back to the bed, spilling onto the floor. "This is the best haul ever. And that was a great idea of yours, getting him to tell you the safe combination."

"Yeah, I know. More than four hundred thousand." Her face turned serious. "We need to stay quiet for awhile. No more runs."

"With all this, we could stop for years." Black Pearl got out of the bed, hundred dollar bills sliding off her, shedding the money from her body, finally exposing a black string bikini. "That was refreshing. Now, it's going to take me all morning to stack this all back into neat piles."

"We're not going anywhere." Blonde Pearl put down the watch. "You think that guy is going to the cops?" She had the expression of a player thinking about the next chess move. "I mean, he didn't have a ring. No honey to hide from. He could go to the police and complain."

"So let him." She snapped the bikini string against her body until it fit just right.

"The problem is, we have some history with the police. Not scary contact, but just enough."

"And you tossed his cell phone?," the blonde asked.

"Dropped it in when we crossed the bridge."

"You sure about the cops? This is a lot of cash."

Black Pearl said, "All they have is a description from our other runs. No photographs, no mugs, nothing. We've never been arrested before. They got nothing. Let'm go to the police." She eased the wig from her head. A short cropped Afro was underneath. The long-locked wig was placed on a styrofoam head. Seven other wigs and heads were lined up on the dresser. "Tomorrow, I can be just as blonde as you," she laughed.

"Still, we've got enough to leave town and be quiet for a long while." She turned her attention to the briefcase. "What do think is in that thing?"

"I don't know but he kept that stupid case closer than his wallet. I mean, he kept talking about it in that stupor."

Blonde Pearl picked up the case. She ran her fingers over the locks. "I wish I knew the numbers to open this. Probably just a bunch of useless paper."

"Why not just get a saw. Cut into it."

"If we have to, we'll get this thing open. Right now, I just want to get in the shower and get a big breakfast."

Red-tipped, ebony fingers selected a wig to wear. All black. “Should we call Stan? I mean, he found this guy for us. We owe him his usual cut.”

Black Pearl pictured Stan at home watching TV, spoon in-hand swirling a bowl of cereal, imbibing in milk rather than tasting one of his brilliant concoctions of Singapore Sling or Tom Collins. Stan was a real home-body who kept true to a schedule of doing nothing unless he had a stake in it.

“We can mail him the cut. We need to get out of town. If he only knew how rich we struck it last night.”

“I’m not going to tell him.” They both laughed. A good laugh that rumbled through their bodies, never letting up, and only getting stronger when they raised up from bent over positions and faced eye to eye.

Chapter 4

Stan Willows lived at the end of the street, quiet and distant from other homes. A car was parked in the driveway. Brent Solar pulled over at least a block from the place. He got out of the car. Inside his pocket, he carried a letter opener he grabbed in the motel office when the clerk wasn't watching. I'm not a violent man, he kept telling himself. But he was pushed too far. And his briefcase was missing.

By now, the buyers would know he was a no-show for the meeting. They would come after him, not stopping until they were given a good explanation or he would be dead within a matter of seconds. Stan was going to lead him back to the briefcase.

The house was surrounded by trees. Brent ran up to a large ficus, its roots long and hugging the ground like snakes. From behind the tree, he stared into a window and saw him. The night man was in the kitchen preparing something to eat. Brent waited until he left the kitchen. He was shorter than Brent, smaller in body structure. An easy matchup if he had to get physical. Rather than try the front, Brent sneaked around to the back door. He kept looking for a dog but found nothing. Ducking under the window, Brent quietly aimed his hand toward the door. He turned the knob. The door was not locked. Brent smiled the smile of a burglar. He kept turning until the door was open about an inch. He waited to see if his target heard him.

Nothing.

Brent softy pushed the door open until there was plenty of room for him to step inside. The night man had moved back inside the house. Brent stood in the kitchen and listened. He held out the letter opener. There was movement in the family room. Seconds later, Brent heard the volume on a television increase. He smiled. The TV would give him enough background noise to cover his steps. Brent stepped ever so quietly toward the next room. The letter opener glistened in the sunlight coming through the window. Another step. He was close enough now to hear the soft chews of someone eating heartily. The sound of the television was getting louder as he approached.

Brent worked out in his mind how he would get the letter opener up to Stan's throat. Get it jammed up tight against an artery. Three more steps and he would be ready to move.

The front door broke open, the lock was not able to stop the thrust from something big. The door was smashed, torn off the jamb. Three large men rushed into the room. All three men were holding guns stacked with suppressors.

Stan dropped his food. Brent stood still in shock.

The man in front was wearing a patch over his right eye. "Drop it, Brent." The voice was mechanical, detached, like someone ordering breakfast. The two men next to Eye Patch Man aimed their weapons at Brent. He dropped the letter opener. "What the-" Stan was cut off.

"Stop talking, Mr. Willows." The mechanical voice moved closer. "Yes, I know your name." He turned his attention to Brent. "Where is it? Where is the briefcase?"

"I'm sorry. I was trying to reach you." Brent heard himself speak. Did he really sound that weak? His voice barely carried across the room. He thought about turning and running. No one can outrun a bullet.

Eye Patch turned to him. His words were dripping in sarcasm. "Sure you were trying to reach me. Is that why you ran off from the motel?"

Brent's hand was shaking. "I was meaning to explain. Something happened. I met these two women. They-"

"Let me guess," the voice started. "They got you drugged up and you lost my briefcase. Is that what you're trying to tell me?" Eye Patch Man glared at Brent.

"Yes, yes. I'm here trying to get it back. I promise." Brent pointed to Stan. "This guy knows where they are. He can tell us."

"Who?" Stan shouted. "I don't know anything."

The Voice smiled and turned to Stan. "Oh, I bet you know everything about these girls, don't you? I mean, you tell us what you know." He looked at Brent. "We've already had to clean up your mess. The other bartender, the motel clerk. All gone. It's all your fault Brent. That pencil in your pants got you in trouble."

"We can get it back." Brent yelled at Stan. "Where are they? Where do they live? We can get it back."

Eye Patch raised his palm to both of them. "I'll do the questioning. Brent, have a seat. You don't want to be too close." The men with the guns moved to each side of

Stan Willows. One man was bald, solid as a barrel full of sand. He kept his gun pointed in Brent's direction. Eye Patch stepped in closer, extending Stan a cell phone. "Dial. I'll talk."

Chapter 5

"I don't like this." Blonde Pearl stared at the line of cars in front of her. "Let's just mail him his usual cut and get out of here."

"He's been too good to us. Could get lost in the mail."

Black Pearl checked herself in a mirror. There was an anxiety in her eyes that wasn't there before. "Sure, the thing gets lost in the mail, he gets pissed and makes a quiet call to the cops. We need to give him some money."

They were turning down A1A, the long stretch of road that lines the coast. From somewhere in the back seat, they heard a cell phone ring. Red tipped fingers searched through a duffle bag. "That's the phone we took from the mark. It's ringing."

"Well, answer it."

"Are you kidding? I should have tossed this thing hours ago."

Blonde Pearl said, "Go ahead, just for kicks, answer it."

Black fingers held the phone up to her head. "Go," she said.

The voice said, "Let me be clear, if you want to see Stan just like you remembered him, please bring the briefcase to his house. Right now."

"Who is this?"

There was a pause. Then a familiar voice. “It’s me.”

“It’s Stan. Sounds like he’s in trouble,” she whispered to her friend driving the car. She put the phone back to her ear. “Stan what is it?”

“Just come. No playn' around. Just come right now with the briefcase.” He sounded out of breath. Scared.

“Sure Stan, we were coming by anyway to give you-” She stopped. “Who else is there?”

The mechanical voice came back on the phone. “You have fifteen minutes or Stan will be a memory.” Dial tone.

“I’m turning around. We’re outta here.” She started to turn the wheel. The passenger reached over. Black hands on white fingers. “We’re not leaving Stan. Is that clear? let’s move. Now.”

They parked two houses down from Stan’s house. Both of them sat in the car, figuring their next move. “He’s gonna tell them all about us,” the passenger said.

“But who is that man?”

“And the thing that gets me is, he never asked about the money. Or the watch. The only thing he wanted was the briefcase.”

They both looked at the case. “What is in this thing?” Black Pearl shook it. Quiet.

Blonde Pearl took her eyes off the road. Stared at the case. “And Stan sounded-?”

“Never heard him sound like that before. I knew something was wrong.” She slapped her thigh with her hand. "We never spoke to him and he knew about the briefcase."

They got out of the car, leaving the briefcase behind with the duffle bag. Black Pearl led, walking the sidewalk. Once they got some twenty yards away, she stopped. "Look at the door. It's gone."

"What?"

"It's gone! Look."

Before them, the front of the house looked like a mouth with two front teeth missing. The door was gone and a gaping rectangle hinted at people inside. "Why don't you stay here. I'll find out what they want. If this all goes south, get in the car."

Blonde Pearl said, "I'm not going to leave you behind."

"Just stay here." Black Pearl walked the rest of the way stopping at the front of the house. A man with a patch over one eye walked out. Just behind him was Stan. And behind him was a large man with a gun pointed at Stan's head.

Eye Patch said, "Now why don't you be a good girl and just give me the briefcase."

"And if I do that, what happens to Stan? What happens to us?"

"Why, you go on your way, merrily ripping off unsuspecting hard-up men." He paused. "Now, where is the briefcase?"

"I think I'll keep it for now. Until you release Stan."

Eye-patch man looked behind her. "Does she have the case?"

"Maybe."

"Maybe?" The voice thundered. "Maybe. Maybe this." He nodded to the Bald Man. All she heard was a soft poof. The top of Stan's hair kicked up with the silent blast. He dropped like a sack of cement. His eyes were wide open, locked in death. She sagged down to the ground, weak in the knees, crumpled by the sight, tears and screams coming from her. She saw two men running in her direction. Black Pearl got up and started running for the car. The driver was again behind the wheel, where she had left the engine running, then she reached over and flung open the door with her right hand. Black Pearl barely made it to the seat when a bullet smashed the window, just missing her head.

She screamed, "Get out of here! Go! Go! Go!"

Blonde Pearl was turning the wheel and burying her foot into the pedal at the same time. The tires were spitting bits of dirt and rock as she straightened up the car after the hard turn. Just outside the car, three bullets kicked up big chucks of dirt. They never heard the shots, only the results. In the rear view mirror, she saw another car driving for them. And there was something else.

The man with the patch stood over Stan and aimed the gun. The shot was too soft to be heard but she saw Stan's body absorb the blast.

Black Pearl wiped away another tear. She yelled at the windshield, "They didn't have to do that. I would have given them the briefcase."

Blonde Pearl jammed her foot on the pedal. "They would have killed us anyway."

Chapter 6

She drove as fast as the street lights allowed, zooming around slow cars, and moving past cars in the fast lane, all the while looking back at the rear view mirror.

"They're still on us," the passenger said. The tears were gone, replaced by a rigid street-wise look of someone with years of experience facing harder times. "Up around Third Lane, I'll grab the duffle bag. Everything is in it, including the case. We'll ditch the car in the middle of street. Cause a roadjam. Then we foot it."

"Then what?"

Blonde Pearl took another hard turn. "Just follow my lead. I've got an idea."

A bullet smashed through the rear window sending shards of glass toward the front seat. They covered up, hands on heads, covering the face. Third Lane was four blocks away.

"We're never going to make it," Blonde Pearl said.

"Keep driving!"

The car roared past a slow moving truck. Blonde Pearl zoomed past, then stayed in front of the truck. "What you are doing?" the passenger screamed. "Get moving."

"They can't shoot us through that truck."

"Well, if they catch up to us, you'll get it in the side of the head."

Third Lane was now a block away. From somewhere far behind them, there was a faint sound of police sirens. The car went half-way through the intersection at One Avenue and Third Lane in Stilton Bay.

Then the car came to a screeching stop.

Both of them got out of the car, the passenger flung the duffle bag over her shoulder. They ran east, heads low, looking for bullets. Three drivers startcd screaming at them as they left the car in the middle of the street. Another flipped a middle finger. A car driver started to follow on foot then gave up when the person in the back seat protested.

They were free.

A block away, the noise of honking horns was a brief memory. Ahead of them, a line of restaurants and shops. The

stores on Third Lane were like a shimmering oasis.

"Where are we going?"

Red tipped fingernails pointed to a small sign near the entrance and an elevator. "There."

They ran under the sign. FRANK TOWER - INVESTIGATIONS.

Chapter 7

The man with the Eye Patch pulled a gun from inside his suit coat and aimed the weapon at Brent Solar. "We only have a few moments. I really hoped this deal would work out."

"It still can."

"Can? You got my men shooting in the street. I've got a clean up crew on the way here right now. Three bodies in one day. That's a lot even for me." The gun was aimed at Brent's head. The black suppressor was inches from his face.

"Please. Think about it. You'll get the briefcase back. And when you do, you're going to need me."

"I've got other experts."

"I'm the one who stole it all. I left no trace of my work. Now when I turn up missing, they'll know and they'll start a trail leading right to you. I need to return to work as though nothing happened."

"You're not making your case stronger. I can get by without you."

"Just try. I embedded a code layer that only I know how to discard. Without me, you'll be months trying to figure it out. Do you have months?" Brent played his last card.

"I gave you all that money and all you had to do is deliver the goods. You had twenty-five million coming your way. Instead, you're trying to get you wick wet."

"I screwed up. They gave me something. Knocked me out. Just think about it. You need my help. You will never get into the briefcase."

Eye Patch smiled. "You sure about that? I have my ways."

"Ways takes time. You need me."

"Trust me. In a few minutes, I can make you talk."

Brent had weighed everything before he made the theft, placing everything in the most secure briefcase he could find. He knew the risks, the chance of going to prison for life, and the money. The upfront money was history. Now he just wanted to remain alive. He had it all planned right down to returning to his job, being part of the investigation if anyone discovered what was missing. The plan was perfect. Right up until he let his guard down. Out hustled by two street pros. He messed up. Now he just waited to be shot between the eyes.

"If. I mean when you get the briefcase, you make any move without me and they will be on you so fast. I set it up so only I can start everything happening."

The gun came back down. "They'll be here in less then five minutes. Let's go."

Chapter 8

Frank Tower rapped his fingers in time with the jazz coming from a small boom box tucked in the corner. Tower sat at his desk, stacked with reports ready to go out to clients. Reports that would mean checks coming back to him. Behind him, the walls were lined with pictures of jazz greats. The window to the office was open so the breeze could filter into the room. He was about to make a few phone calls when the door swung open.

Two women burst into the room, one carrying a duffle bag. Both of them winded. The one with blonde hair ran to the window and closed up the window and blinds.

"Can I help you?" Frank Tower was standing now, trying to get a read on the situation. The woman near the blinds stepped away from the window.

Almost out of breath, she was able to get out the words, "We want to hire you. Now!"

"Hire me? To do what?"

The other one clutched the briefcase tight against her body. "If you don't help us, they'll kills us."

"What?" Tower yelled.

"You heard her, we'll die."

"Please, sit down. Tell me what's going on." Tower walked over, and turned off the music, then took out a white legal pad and placed it in front of him.

The one with the duffle spoke through clenched teeth. "We don't have time for this. Get your ass in gear and help us. Now!"

Tower put out his hands in a calming gesture. "Okay, let's start with this. What is your name?"

The one near the window started first. "That's a funny one and we don't have time for the story but my name is Pearl. And guess what? Her name is also Pearl. We're the Pearls-"

Tower smacked the pad on the table. "You two come in here yelling about being in danger, needing my help and then you start off by giving me fake names? We're done. There's the door, or if you want, I can call the police."

"No," both of them yelled in unison. The duffle carrier placed the bag on the floor. "Okay. My name is Wanda. Wanda Philpot. That's Ruanne Stanner. Everybody calls her Ru."

"Okay, Ru and Wanda. What is this all about?"

"We're being followed," Wanda said. She looked down at her brown fingers. A nail was broken.

Ru said, "Yeah, being chased. And we just saw our friend get killed. We took off and they've been following us." Three times Wanda returned to the window and searched the street. "And they're shooting at us."

Tower reached for his cell phone. Both women rushed to Tower smothering his hands, trying to stop him from making the call.

"You don't understand. These aren't your normal people." Wanda looked back at the duffle.

Tower said, “You pay a lot of attention to the duffle bag. What’s in it?”

“Death,” Ru said.

Their words were settling into Tower. He studied them and the situation they described. He wanted to call his friend on the force, let him know the facts presented to him and sort out the truth. They sounded legit. And scared. From his years on the force and before that, life in the street, gave him a strong B-S meter.

Tower said, “We’re going to get out of here. Get to a place I think is safe. We’ll have another conversation about what happened. I won’t call the police. For now. But you’ve got to be honest with me. Did you do something illegal?”

Both of them stared at him. Wanda let out a small laugh.

“Let me change that,” Tower said. “If it’s something illegal and I don’t report it, I could lose my license. Maybe obstruction of justice tossed in for good measure.” He pulled his Glock from his desk drawer and pressed it behind him, tucked away in his jeans. “Let’s go.”

Tower reached for the duffle. She hesitated at first. Tower looked into her eyes. There was genuine fear there. He reached out his hand. Her fingers were trembling. Finally, she turned over the duffle bag to Tower. They followed him out the door. He locked up, then directed them toward the stairs. They would take the back way out. No front door. Just before they were about to leave, Tower motioned for them to wait. He carefully approached the tinted glass front door and studied the street. No strange faces. He walked back to the women and was the first out of the back door. Tower checked the back lot. All seemed normal.

They followed him to his car. No words spoken. Just a quick exit from the building. He thought for a moment and came up with the perfect place to hide them. Still he had to do something first.

Chapter 9

Tower knew Derreck Rock didn't like people just showing up at his place. This, however, was a different situation. Derreck was a good man, and a great investigator. He had his own PI business and when Tower had too much to do, he would outsource some of the work to Rock. The client didn't need to know who did the surveillance, just as long as someone did the work. He held on to the car key and kept the two in the car.

During the car ride, the two explained everything. Ru spilled about being the one to set up the mark once they got information from Stan. Yes, it was illegal but at this point they did not care anymore. Tower took it all in, listening intently, just as he once did on the police force, hearing stories from perps. In ten minutes, they were there. He walked up to the house, knocked and rang the bell. He heard footsteps from somewhere inside.

"Yeah, yeah, what is it?" Rock shouted at the door. The door opened. "Oh, Frank, it's you. I was about to rip someone a new one."

Tower entered without an invitation. "I need a favor. A big one. And I can't provide a lot of details. At least not yet."

"Sure. What do you want done?"

"I need you to check out the story of two people." Tower explained all the details as he knew them. The possible bar killing. The death of the second bar tender at his home. The locations and the circumstances. Tower could trust him. Still he stared at Tower. "What is this all about?"

"I can't say just yet." Tower shrugged his shoulders.

"Frank, you're the best private insurance investigator I know. This doesn't sound anything like insurance fraud."

"I promised them I would help."

"Them?"

"Forget about it. They're running scared. Just let me know if their story checks out. And I need the information as soon as possible."

"No problem. I'm on it as soon as you leave. Just one question. Why not go to the police on this one?"

"I can't involve them just yet. I need more facts."

Tower shook his hand, then let himself out of the house. the next stop would be tougher.

Chapter 10

Tower studied his two car guests when he wasn't looking down the road. "You two been arrested before?"

"Never," Wanda said.

Ru shifted in her seat. "You think we're street girls. We don't prostitute."

"And we've never been booked." Wanda was staring the skin off Frank's face.

"You mean never been booked, yet." Frank directed his words at the windshield.

"You said you didn't want to know about anything bad." Wanda's stare cooled.

Tower gripped the wheel. "I could get in trouble. But in this case, I think I want to know everything."

"Where are you taking us?" Ru asked.

"Somewhere safe."

They kept driving through the outskirts of Stilton Bay. The well prepared store windows were left behind blocks ago. All the pressure cleaned streets of downtown were miles back. They had crossed over the tracks. "You know where we are?" Tower asked.

Wanda looked around at the surroundings. Two houses were boarded up with a bank notice on the front door, evidence of foreclosure. "What do they call this place again?"

"T Town," Tower replied. "All the street names here begin with the letter T."

The more they drove, the more Ru's eyes got larger. They passed a prostitute with a torn blouse, skinned right knee, scuffed up high heels and a smile for Wanda and Ru as if giving them mutual respect. Ru frowned back. "When are we going to stop?"

"Soon. Just two more blocks."

The place rested in the shadow of the busy I-95 expressway, in the middle of a grouping of banyan trees, mixed with tall bending palms. The cars above on the expressway were up many feet above the building and the concrete and guardrail structure was like a giant wall. Tower pulled up at the one-story building, out of sight from the eyes of tourists and drivers.

"What is this?" Wanda demanded.

Tower pointed to the place. "This is the Never Too Late. Drug rehabilitation."

"We're not addicts," Ru shot back.

"I don't think anyone will find you here. There's a place in the back."

Tower drove to the back parking lot and parked in the shade of a fifty-foot tall ficus tree. There were dried leaves all over the lot. The surrounding plants made the area look like a jungle, with huge split-leaf philodendron, and untamed

cherry hedge. Tower got out of the car and waited.

A woman walked out of the back door. Her hair was a nice color of gray. The fingernails were short and not painted, the hands heavily veined, long streaks of wrinkles marked the face and there was a band-aide on her right arm. The eyes were brown with a hint of broken veins in the whites. And she looked angry. Very angry.

Ru and Wanda got out of the car, stretching out the tight fitting jeans. Wanda took her hands to smooth down the wig.

"Wanda, Ru, meet Jackie. She owns and runs the Never Too Late."

"Good to see you, Frank. I told you about coming around here unannounced."

"I know Jackie, but this is important." He paused a moment to catch her attention but she was focused on the two figures standing in the dappled sunlight.

"Frank, you look like you need something. You here to ask me something?" Jackie never took her eyes off the two women.

"I need your extra place."

Three, four seconds passed before she answered. "No one is in there."

"Good," Tower said. "Then we'll take it."

"We?" The word rolled from Jackie's lips like something repugnant.

"Just for a couple of days." Tower moved directly in front of Jackie to get her looking at him. "Then we're out of here."

"Two days. With those two?" She pointed at Ru and Wanda. "If you're trying to get back with Shannon, this is a fine way to show it."

"No, it's not that way. This is business."

"Sure it is." Jackie gave a sarcastic smile.

"Shannon doesn't need to know," Tower said.

"She'll find out. She always does. And when she does, she'll cut you off for good."

"Can we stay?" Tower asked again.

"You know I can't say no to you. Let me get the keys."

She disappeared into the building. Deep inside the place, Frank knew those recovering were inside. She didn't want him around because he still looked so much like a cop. That made her people nervous. Jackie returned and handed him the key. "Two days," she said. "I'm doing this for my Frankie." Then she was gone.

"It's this way." He pointed to a path.

Wanda tried not to fall in the tall heels, stumbling on the scattering of wet branches and twigs on the ground. Ru now carried the briefcase. Wanda held a tight grip on the duffle. Tower thought about offering to carry one or the other but gave up the idea after seeing the hard looks he got. The back residence was a small house, tucked away in a gathering of ficus trees and one very tall banyan. The temperatures were cooler with all the constant shade. Tower slipped in the key and the door yawned open to smells of stale air.

"Great," Ru said to no one in particular. She crinkled her nose as she entered the place. "Smells like some old wet socks."

Wanda went straight to the bedrooms, sticking her head in each of them before making an announcement. "I've got the room with no windows." She placed the duffle bag on the bed but did not let go.

Tower stared at her. "You taking that thing to the restroom with you?"

"Yes."

Ru found the room with two windows, both covered with heavy shades. "I like it."

"Where you sleeping?" Wanda asked Tower.

"He can sleep in my room," Ru smiled.

"I'll be on the couch. By the door."

"If you change your mind, sweetheart, just come on in. I'll leave the door open."

"How long do you think we'll have to be cooped in here?" Wanda said, inspecting a small closet.

"It all depends. I've got someone checking things out and I want my tech guy to come over and look at that briefcase."

"Another person? How many people you gonna tell about us?" Wanda's voice had a hard edge.

"Just Tray. His name is Tray Colby. He does everything for me that's technical. I want him to look at the briefcase. You can trust him."

Wanda walked back into the middle of the living room. She stared back at the duffle bag then turned to Tower. "Who was that woman, what's her name, Jackie? She a friend?"

Tower paused a few moments. "She's my mother."

"Mother..." Wanda was taking in the word. "And you call her Jackie instead of mom or mother?"

"It's a long story," Tower opened up one of the windows and turned up the air-conditioning to a cooler level. From somewhere outside, they heard the loud hum of the unit. Cool air kicked in from the vents. "I'll open this window for twenty minutes. Get the stale out. Then close it up. It should be cool soon."

Wanda did not want to give up her line of questioning. "Was Jackie a..."

"Addict? Yes. She still considers herself in recovery." Tower's words spewed out of him like confession. "Did it ruin my childhood? Almost. Did I live with her? Yes. Was she around to care for me? No. Did she leave me home alone for days at a time when I was just six? Yes. Did I find her in an alley once almost dead? Yes. Should I go on?"

"You don't have to. I'm sorry."

"Sorry for what? I turned out okay. Made it to the force for six years. Left on my own accord, started up my PI business. I'm doing fine."

Ru stepped closer, still holding the briefcase. "And Shannon?"

Tower closed the window rather than letting it stay open for the twenty minutes he promised. He started to leave, then turned back at them. "I screwed up. Almost ruined everything." Tower sat down in the lumpy folds of the couch. "I had an affair." He punched a bulge in the couch until it was flat. "Had an affair with one of my clients. Shannon found out."

Ru placed the briefcase down and sat next to him. "That's okay. We all make mistakes."

"I can't believe you said that." Wanda put both hands on her hips.

Ru reached out and placed her arm on the top of the couch. "I'm here to listen, sweetheart. Anytime."

"Then my mistress was murdered."

Ru stopped the movement of her arm. "She was what?"

"We got the bastard. That part is over. But Shannon and I..."

“So Shannon is your wife?” Wanda said.

“Yes. But we haven’t been together in months. She’s still trying to decide if she’s going to go through with a divorce.” Tower wiped down his face. After a few minutes he looked at the both of them.

“So, you’re kinda free?” Ru was looked up and down at Tower.

“Unfortunately, yes. For the moment.”

Ru pointed to the bedroom. “Sweetheart, I’ll take you tonight and a bath towel in the morning and I’ll be just fine.”

Wanda gave her a hard stare. A stare with a full meaning of we’re in danger, about to lose our lives and you’re trying to get laid.

For the first time since Tower had a moment to really look at Ru and Wanda.

Ru had that great accent, definitely southern and almost always flirtatious. The blue eyes rested on cheeks looking soft as rose petals. Her gaze was infectious and her figure perfect. Still, Tower knew there was a brain working full-time to get the best angle for her and for Wanda. The good looks were a cover like a magician directing the audience to look somewhere else while the slight-of-hand was being done right in front of them.

Wanda’s brown eyes never stopped roaming. She maintained a quick mind, and seemed to be the one who could reel in Ru when she went too far. There was a secret behind those eyes, Tower thought. A secret on why the two paired up to steal. He had to be careful, reasoning they both knew how to push the charm and maneuver a man. Tower realized he was staring at them longer than he wanted.

A few moments of awkward silence was finally interrupted by Tower. “So, now you know a lot about me. Again, what happened?”

“We like to hunt,” Wanda said.

“Hunt?”

Ru looked down at the stains on the carpet. “That’s what we call it. Hunting. We hunt for marks. We stake out men with money, nice watches, drug them and...” Ru stopped.

Wanda urged her on. “Tell him. We steal every dime they have. Sometimes we screw’m for kicks. Whatever fits our mood.”

“Is that what happened here?”

“Yes. But we didn’t mean for anyone to get hurt.” Ru was making a circle motion with her toe. “We had no idea this guy would have this much money.” She opened the duffle exposing the many stacks of cash.

“Or this stupid briefcase.” Wanda added.

“How many people have you...hunted down?”

Wanda said, “At last count, twenty-seven in three states. We move around if it gets too hot.”

There was a knock at the door. Wanda and Ru jumped. “Come in,” Tower yelled.

Jackie walked into the center of the room with four bags. “Dipped into my wallet. Bought you all some food. You’ll find po’ boy sandwiches, some fries and some drinks. Hope you don’t mind a po’ boy.”

“Thanks Jackie.” Tower took the bags from her.

Jackie took notice of the hard stares from Wanda and Ru. She turned to Tower. "You been telling them about me?"

"Just a bit. Not much." Tower handed over the food to waiting hands.

"Don't sugarcoat it, Frankie. I was the world's worst mother. The only thing I cared about was my drug. Crack all day and all night." She pointed to Tower. "He came last. If I thought I could score, I left him in a crack-cocaine second." For a brief moment, the three of them could see Jackie pondering her past. She stared off at an empty section of the room. "I stole money, burglarized homes, forgot about meals. Did what I could to get my drugs, morning, noon and night. Drugs, drugs, drugs. It was the only thing that was important."

"You don't have to get into all this." Tower took the last meal and placed it on the arm of the couch.

"I want to talk about it. I have to talk about it. It's my duty now to only speak the truth. No more lies. No more hiding behind the crack. That's the message I tell my people. I wasn't there for Frankie. But I can be here for him now, and the people in my program. Now, I know what's important."

Jackie stared into the faces of Ru and Wanda. "I'm not going to ask you what's going on here. I'm not here to judge. Trust me, I don't have the right to judge anyone. Just be careful."

Tower turned to her. "Jackie, I can say-"

She held up her palms to Tower as if to say stop. "No more. It's part of your business and I trust you." She left closing the door with a soft thud. She was gone.

Tower’s cell rang. “Yes.”

It was Derreck Rock. “We have to talk. Where can we meet?”

Chapter 11

"What do you mean, nothing there?" Wanda walked around the carpet in circles, hands on her hips, staring every few seconds at the duffle then rearranging her hair. "I need to change my wig. Left all of them in the car. We have no clothes. Nothing." She turned to Derreck Rock, who was sitting on a depression in the deep couch. "There had to be something."

"I went to the bar. Everything looked normal. I went inside. No police investigation. Nothing. People eating. Drinking. I asked at the bar and the guy told me he was new. A temp. That everyone else called in sick."

"Sick? Do you believe that?" Ru took kept shifting her legs. "There had to be someone there."

Rock continued. "I went to the address you told me. It all looked quiet."

"What about the door?" Wanda shouted at him.

"The door was there. In place. No police tape. No investigation. I walked around twice. Looked in the window. No body. Nothing. Everything in the room looked neat. The house checked out fine."

"That's impossible." Wanda was flinging her arms at the ceiling. "We saw a man get killed. Saw him drop. Bullets flying at us."

"I checked the street. I looked around. Believe me, if there was anything there, I would know it. No bullet casings. It was all quiet. Checked with some people on the force. No reports of anything. No one reported hearing anything. Either at the bar or the house."

Ru sat in a chair listening, then stacked and unstacked her legs. "What about our car? We left it in the middle of the intersection."

"No car. I asked all around. The best I could come up with is a guy at a restaurant says a tow truck came up really fast and towed the thing out of there. Life went on. There is no trace of anything you told me."

Ru stood up and stared at Tower. "So now you don't believe us?"

"Could they be that professional? Able to clean up a house, fix the door and clear away an accident. Maybe." Tower tried to sound reasonable.

Wanda went to the duffle, pulled out a stack of hundreds and aimed them in the direction of Tower and Rock. "And what do you call this? This just didn't drop out of the sky. And the briefcase. Someone is after us. Tried to kill us."

"I don't understand this," Ru said. "The only thing I know is that our friend is dead and we are in danger."

"I believe you." Tower got out a small writing pad. "Who else knows about your activities."

"No one," Ru said.

Tower turned to Derreck. "Thanks for your help. You've got a lot to do, we'll take it from here."

"No problem," he said. "Let me know if you still need my help." Rock left the house.

Tower again turned to them. “I didn’t want you to tell all in front of him. Now, in your hunting as you call it, what do you do with the jewelry?”

Wanda smacked the side of her leg. “I forgot. Our fence. And he’s a good one. Gives us fifty percent on everything we bring him.”

Ru’s face took on the look of someone who just remembered something terrible. “He could be in trouble. If they continue to track our movements, they’ll find him at some point.”

“How do you reach him?”

“He doesn’t have a phone,” Wanda said. “We go to a post office box and leave a message, listing a certain time. He shows up. We do business. Give him the stuff. Usually watches and rings. Gives us an estimate. Pays us on the spot.” She thought for a moment. “Damn,” she muttered.

“What?” Tower said.

Ru said, “In all this, we forgot. We left him a message to meet us later today at Stilton Bay park. We have this.” Ru reached into the duffle and pulled out the Rolex.

“Wow,” Tower said, examining the watch. “Nice. Did it belong to Solar?”

“Yes” Ru said. “Probably has his prints on it.”

“We’ll hold on to it. Who else knows anything about you two?”

“Just our building manager.” Wanda’s face grew grim. “We’re putting a lot of people in a bad way.”

“The guys behind this are going out of their way to cover up their tracks. They must have a clean up crew.

The building manager might be a low priority. What they want right now is you."

There was a knock at the door.

Chapter 12

Tray Colby winced at the sight of the room. Cramped quarters. Two women. One with torn black stockings, high heels and now wearing super-cutoff jean shorts. The other kept tugging at a wig.

"You sure this is the last person you're gonna bring over here? I feel like I'm on display." Wanda would not stop walking in a small circle.

Tray reached into a black bag and pulled out a power drink, opening the small can and in a matter of seconds, devoured the entire contents. He tossed the empty in the bag and pulled out another.

"Sweetheart, you keep that up and you're gonna need a gym to work it off."

"I'm fine." Tray opened the drink and placed it on the small kitchen table. "Now," he announced. "Where is it?"

Tower nodded to Ru to bring the briefcase. She placed it on the table, almost tipping over the power drink. "Wow," Colby said. "You weren't kidding. This is fantastic." Tray reached into his bag and pulled out a pair of plastic gloves, snapping them on and taking a swig of the drink. Tray resembled a lab tech examining a rare specimen. He carefully spun the case around, studying the hinges and the front of the case. He took a tiny flashlight and pointed the beam toward the front of the case. "Who held this first?"

Ru raised her hand.

"And when you walked away, did you get a shock?"

"No. Why?"

Tray moved back a bit from the case, sighed and addressed the three of them. "What you have here is a very sophisticated briefcase with some of the best security measures I've ever seen. First, you could drop this thing from a five story building and it wouldn't open. Run a truck over it twenty times or more and you'd get the same thing. This is stronger than an elephant's armpits."

Tray aimed a gloved index finger toward two glass-inch squares, both green in color. "You see these? These are both recognition cards."

"What?" Ru said.

Tower was standing behind her. "You need a body part to open the thing."

Tray continued. "This first one here, this is a fingerprint scanner. You need the right print to get it open. But that's just the start. You see the other one?"

Both Ru and Wanda leaned in. "That ladies, is an eye scanner. Optical recognition. And trust me, I doubt if you have either."

"And the shock?" Ru asked again.

"Well, some of these cases come with an element like something out of the movies. You take the case and walk off a certain distance and blam, you get a shock. Just enough to make you drop the case."

Tower asked. "Well, can you open it?"

"There are two ways. One, you can find the person with the eye and finger to open this thing. Or you can let me try and cut. I can get my hands on a plasma torch and burn right through the hinges. The only problem with that is whether this thing is booby trapped or I could accidentally burn what's inside."

Tower said, "We can't do number one and right now our only option is number two. Ru, Wanda, it's your case. What do you want to do?"

"We torch it," both of them said in unison.

"Torch, it is. Give me three hours and I'll hook back up with you." Tray swigged the rest of the drink, got up from the table and pulled a third can from his bag as he left the tight confines of the house. Tower followed him down the path to the parking lot.

"Okay, how did you connect with them?" Tray looked at the can then put it back in his black bag.

"They ran into the office, saying they had just witnessed a murder. A bar tender who sets up some of their hunts."

"Hunts?"

"That's the same response I had. They rip off men in bars. Drug them out of their minds after teasing them into bed."

"The tease part I can understand. They both have great legs."

"This is serious Tray. I believe them. If they're running away from some pros who can clean up this well, I'm not sure what they got themselves into. And they say the people on the phone weren't even interested in the money. Just the briefcase."

"Let me see if I can cut that time in half. Say, meet back here in an hour or so."

Ru stared through the window. "They're out there talking about us."

Wanda put the money back into the duffle. "I say we blow this place. Get out of here and get on the road. Buy a car and keep driving west. No California. Say Nebraska or Iowa."

"Us in Middle America? You know we need to be on a coast somewhere. I like this Tower guy. We need his help right now."

Chapter 13

Tower was about to open the door when his cell phone rang. The number on his cell belonged to Detective Mark David. Tower let the phone ring three times. He ignored it. The call went to voice mail but no message was left on the phone. Decision time. What could Mark want? He was thinking about whether to call him back when the phone rang again. Mark again. Tower picked up.

"Yes."

"Frank, it's Mark. Where are you?"

"Somewhere. Why?"

"We need to talk."

"I'm kind of tied up right now. On a project."

"Frank, how long have I known you?"

"Long time. All six years on the force, and since I opened up the office. Mark, what's going on?"

"We need to sit down. Better yet, you need to come in."

"Mark, this sounds official rather than social. I can't come into the station right now."

"I thought I would reach out to you first. I went by the office and no one was there. But I'm asking you, please come into the Stilton Bay police office in one hour."

"I'm sorry Mark. I can't do that. Not until you tell me what is going on."

"Okay, here goes. Your name has been flagged."

"What are you saying?"

There was a long pause. "Frank, your name is on a red flag from Homeland Security. People are looking for you."

"Why?"

"I don't know. There's going to be a short briefing in one hour. All I know is they are looking for you for some reason. You're not going to be able to fly anywhere or leave this country, you understand."

Tower looked back at the house. He felt like the place was about to fall on him. His thoughts swirled around the two people who first called themselves Pearls. The two mystery women with tales of a man killed, concern about anyone working at the bar, enough money to buy up a block of houses and the briefcase. Tower considered telling all on the phone. Just give it up and spew everything he knew about Ru and Wanda. Still, they hired him to protect them. He wasn't even sure if that was the reason for the national attention on himself but he wouldn't give up the two so-called hunters. Not yet. Tower reached a decision.

"I can't come in right now. I seem to be in the middle of something and I have to figure out what I'm going to do."

"You sure about this? I was hoping we could work this out. You're my best friend. I was in your wedding. There is still time to turn this into your favor. Just come on in."

"I can't. Trust me on this. I have to work it out."

Tower ended the call. In his conversation, there was no mention of the women. For his entire professional life, Tower was also a hunter. A hunter of thugs, burglars and killers when he was on the force. Later, he was the hunter of cheaters of the insurance system. He was a hired gun by companies or anyone who suspected someone skirting the law.

Now, he was being hunted.

Tower didn't like the feeling. He stepped into the house. Wanda and Ru both looked worried.

"Our phone has been going off," Wanda said.

"Phone?"

"The one we took from Brent Solar."

Chapter 14

Wanda extended the phone to Tower. The three of them watched and listened as the phone rang again. Tower picked up but did not say anything, opting instead to put the voice on speaker.

"Please don't hang up. It's too important," the voice said.

Tower put the phone on the kitchen table, took out his pad and wrote in large letters: YOU RECOGNIZE THE VOICE.

Wanda took the pad from his and wrote down, the man with the patch on the pad. Tower nodded. They kept listening.

Eye Patch said, "I know you escaped from us but we hope to remedy that in the next few hours. Please, you know what I want. Just give me the briefcase and this can all go away."

All three stood motionless in the tiny kitchen. Tower listened and let the voice sink in so he would always remember the tonality. "If you don't think we mean what we say, then I've got a few, shall we say, surprises for you."

There was a pause. Eye Patch continued. "Wanda and Ru. Yes, that's right we know your names. Your dead departed friend was kind enough to let us know all he could before he was no longer a part of the picture. Keep listening, Mr. Tower."

Frank thought about getting his Glock from his

car. Right now, the man had all of his attention. "That's right, Mr. Frank Tower. It took awhile but we managed to trace their steps after the car was left in the intersection. Right up to your office, Mr. Tower. But I have something for you to think about. Please, if you can, find a laptop or a computer please."

Frank had a lap with him, along with some paperwork and the legal pad. He turned it on.

"If you would, please to go this website address. Since you have not hung up, I can only think you are still with us, Mr. Tower."

Frank listened to the man and looked up the web site he was given. The long collection of numbers and letters was unlike anything he had ever seen. Once there, there was a blue dot in the middle of the screen.

"Now, if you would, please click on the dot."

Tower did has he was instructed. Wanda, Ru and Tower stared at the computer screen. The dot dissolved away and now they were watching what looked like bushes. A hedge. Up close. The camera was sending them streaming video of a cherry hedge.

The voice on the phone spoke again. "Keep watching. What you are seeing is live. Our subject has no idea we are there."

The three of them continued to watch as the camera angle moved from the hedge and now showed the back yard of a house. Tower recognized the place immediately.

"That's Shannon's house. Get your men away from there now!" Tower's hand came down so hard on the table, Wanda had to grab the laptop as it bounced and almost slid to the floor.

"Ah, Mr. Tower. You are there. Now I have your undivided attention. I'm guessing we are all assembled and watching? That's good."

Tower's words came out hard and slow, each one punctuated by anger. "Get your people back from there right now."

"Or what? Something will happen to me? You don't even know who I am. Or what I am capable of doing."

"If anything happens to her..."

Veins in Tower's neck bulged. His fists were tight and strong as mallets. The muscles in his arms tightened.

"Keep watching," the voice on the phone commanded. As they watched, they saw Shannon through the large glass windows, step into the room, her figure stepping lightly about the room, letting her robe drop to the floor, exposing her back and bra straps to the camera. She then eased off her shorts sliding them effortlessly down a curved body until they dropped at her feet. Next came the bar. Her backside was naked for just a few seconds as she stepped into a bathing suit, and pulled on the straps until she seemed comfortable with the fit. Shannon moved the sliding glass doors apart and stepped into the shade of her patio.

"Stop this. Now." Tower was screaming at the phone. "Stop."

"Why stop. I'm enjoying this. She's very beautiful, Mr. Tower."

"Pull your men out now."

"Everything that happens next depends on you. Give me the briefcase. We will let all of you go your merry way. Just give me the briefcase."

"Who are you? And why the case?" Tower tried one last attempt to gain information.

"Mr. Tower, you are in no position to bargain or ask questions. Give me what I want. If I don't get it back, I have six men stationed all around her house. Six large, eager men who would just love to get better acquainted with your lovely friend. And she is beautiful. Just keep thinking about that Mr. Tower. Six men."

"I will kill you." Tower's words were flat and purposeful.

"No you won't. And if you go anywhere near her, if you contact the police, or any authorities, I will know about it. I must hear from you by noon tomorrow. If I don't hear from you, my men will move in. And believe me, Mr. Tower, when they are done with her, there won't be anything left."

The screen went blank.

Chapter 15

"Just do as I say." Tower took an empty food bag and opened it wide, ready for items to be tossed in. "I want your cell phones, anything that might give off a GPS signal. I want them now."

Wanda removed her seldom used cell phone and placed it in the bag. He turned to Ru. She also collected her cell, seven-teen credit cards and a library card. "Everything has to go. Let me guess," Tower said, "the cards are hot?"

"Even the library card." Wanda sat down next to her duffle bag. "I'm sorry your wife got mixed up in this."

"Don't be sorry, just think. Is there any other connection to you other than the ones you mentioned?"

"No." Ru stared at the briefcase. "What is in this thing?" She shook it up. Nothing.

Tower checked his watch. "Tray will be back here soon. I'll be right back. We don't need three people on the road right now. I'll get rid of the phones." Tower ran to his car. Even Brent Solar's phone was in the bag. Wanda removed her wig and rested it on the table. For the first time, Tower saw the rounded top of her Afro and wondered why she didn't wear it like that all the time. In the same instant, he remembered they were putting on a show for their targets. The hair, the look, the tease all went into the game for find another victim in a bar.

When Tower left the tiny house, his two guests were busy making the place comfortable. He drove past the rehabilitation center, spitting rocks and dried Roseapple Tree leaves. He kept going until he reached a bridge over the Intracoastal Waterway. Tower placed Wanda's cell phone on a truck parked nearby with Indiana state plates. He tossed another in a garbage bin when he heard the collection truck lumbering down the street headed for his location. The hit credit cards also went in. Brent Solar's phone went into the Intracostal waters, landing with a soft splash. He saved his own phone for last.

Then he headed back.

Tower parked the car and rushed inside the house. He knew immediately something was different. Tower called out but there was no one inside. He walked a quick pace back to the parking lot. Jackie was waiting for him.

"If you're looking for the girls, they're gone."

Tower leaned against his car, his mind swirling of thoughts on what should be his next move. Inside the house, the duffle and briefcase were also gone.

"Did they say where they were going?"

"No. Just that they said 'Don't worry about them.' But I think your girlfriends are in a lot of trouble." Jackie moved in closer to him. "They just got into a cab and headed back downtown."

"I've got to tell you something." Tower pulled out four hundred dollars in cash, extending the money toward Jackie. "Take this," he said. Tower always kept a nice stash of get-away money in his front left pocket.

"I can't take your money."

"Take it."

"No. Not gonna take your money." She took two steps away from him. Tower only moved closer to her. Jackie rubbed her eyes. "Look, you know why I can't take that money. I abandoned you so many times where you were a child. I used you as a front to steal from people, I lied to everyone I ever knew." She paused. For a quick moment, Tower thought Jackie might let the tears flow. She straightened up. No tears. "Frankie, it's a wonder you survived. With the stuff I did, you should have been dead."

"Jackie..."

"No. I have to let it out. My counseling style means you tell everything. Get everything out. Don't hold back. I almost killed you, Frankie. At times, I left you with strangers. Once I stole the money you got for a birthday from your father and I spent it on crack. I took everything I had and used it on drugs. I'm not a good person and now I have to spend the rest of my life getting others off the demon."

"You're helping a lot of people."

"It's not enough." She looked upward at the powder blue sky. "Up there, they know it's not enough. But I'm trying. I try everyday."

"Look, I have to go. You won't see me for awhile."

Jackie's eyes were again trained on Tower.

"I could be in some trouble. If anyone comes around looking for me, you don't know where I am and I'm not going to tell you. So here, take this money."

"You keep it. I'll get along. And Heaven knows, anyone messes with me will be in a stinkpot of hurt."

Tower put the money back in his pocket. "Be careful. I don't think they will come by here but there are some people looking for me."

"I'll be just fine. Go. Do what you have to do. I know those girls are part of the problem. I just know it."

Jackie looked into Tower's face.

"Why can't they just be more like Shannon."

Chapter 16

Tower met Tray Colby as he drove into the parking lot. Tray's expression changed as he got out of the van. "They're gone, aren't they?"

"And they took the briefcase with them." Tower was wearing a sport coat to hide the gun holster. "I'm on the hotseat. I'm not sure exactly what trouble I'm in but after this, you better get as far away from me as possible."

Tray studied Tower. "You know I won't agree to that. If you need me, I'm there. What do you need?"

"These people are organized and very capable. They have a camera on Shannon and promise to kill her if I don't deliver the briefcase to them by noon tomorrow."

Tray opened up his van and sat on the floorboard. "Okay. What else they got?"

"Somehow I'm on a Homeland Security watch. I think these people are setting me up but I don't know how they're doing it. I think the girls took off because they think I'll sell them out in order to protect Shannon. But I wouldn't do that."

"How can I help?"

"I dumped my phones, my laptop, everything. These guys have the ability to track IP addresses and probably in time, track down cell phone pings off towers and trace numbers."

Tower pointed to the house. "I left the door open. Use your stuff to dust for prints. Maybe they're in a system. You know how to check the prints-"

"Trust me," Tray said, "I'll take care of the prints. Anything else?"

"They left DNA all over the place. Swab what you need. Also, black Pearl, Wanda. She likes wigs. I noticed in her purse, she had a business card with MANBY WIGS. Check for a store selling Manby. They are carrying a ton of money. They don't have any clothes. Right now they are probably planning where to spend some of that cash to buy dresses, a car, and maybe someone with a cutting torch to open up that case."

"I'm on it," Tray said. He looked over at the rehab center. "She going to be okay?"

"I think she'll be fine."

Tray moved inside his van. Tower heard a series of drawers being opened. Stuff being moved around. Tray reappeared with a phone-like device.

Tower said, "I don't want to take your satellite phone."

"Take it. You need it. And I've got these." He handed Tower three cell phones. "These are throw-aways. Burners. Use them a few times and toss'm. Use the sat phone as a last resort or in an emergency. I've got it set up so the source location is protected."

"Thanks. And I'll need some more weapons."

"No problem. Got you covered." Tray leaned into the van and pulled out a duffle bag. "Check them out later. Not here. But you'll be happy."

"I don't know how to thank you."

"What do you know about these women?"

Tower paused. "We didn't have time to fill out the regular paperwork. I don't have an social security number, address. Nothing. I did a quick search. They're right, they've never been arrested. I just need more info."

Tray scanned the lot. "The only thing I can't get you is a different car."

"Don't worry, I've got something in mind." Tower snapped his fingers. "I need two more favors."

"I'm all ears."

"First, get in touch with Derreck. Don't tell him anything but just let him know not to try and reach me for awhile. If you're over this way, look in on Jackie." Tower grabbed the duffle bag. "This one is not full of money." He smiled. "But the briefcase. That is what is bothering me. I managed to do a quick check on Brent Solar."

"And?"

"Couldn't find much. His background is probably protected. But it did say that he was an outside contractor, specializing in computers."

"I'll do some digging as well."

Tower put the duffle in his other hand. "I have to work fast. Can't go back to my office since it's probably being watched. My apartment is off limits as well. I've got to become a ghost."

Tray closed up the van. "If you need me, you know how to reach me."

Tower nodded. "Thanks. I'm going hunting."

Chapter 17

Detective Mark David hesitated before going into the police building. He stood under the branches of a large Maple tree, secure in the shade and away from the broil of a June heat in Stilton Bay. David gathered up a few files and was prepared to close his car door.

The ping of a small rock hit his fender and the detective turned around but did not see anyone. He again re-stacked the files under his arm and was about to turn toward the front doors when he heard a second ping. This time hitting the roof of his car.

"Alright, this isn't funny. Whose out there?"

A few seconds of silence. "Is the best man at my wedding going to lock me up?" The sound came from a couple of cars over.

"Tower? That you? Where you are you?"

"Don't look in my direction. I don't have a lot of time and I don't want to end up in your jail cell. Why am I being flagged?"

Mark David spoke to the general area where the voice was coming from. "All they want is to talk to you. There are no arrest warrants. No searches. But they want to speak to you about the deposit."

"Deposit?"

"Yes. You don't know?"

"Please Mark, I've been too busy to check."

"Well, if you did, you'd see your accounts have

been frozen. They're trying-" He paused. "Why don't we just go upstairs and we can talk about this."

"No way. I've got too many things up in the air. I go in there and won't come out for five years. What deposit?"

"We really need to bring you in."

"This is one time when I'm pleading with you. Mark, you have to trust me on this. Let me figure this out a bit first, then I promise I will sit down with you or anyone else."

"Your account took on a deposit two days ago of more than one-hundred-sixty thousand dollars. Any idea what that's about?"

"I have no idea. And of course, anything over ten thousand-"

Mark finished the sentence, "Gets the attention of the feds. It came from an off-shore account. They only told me so much. But they are very concerned about the source of the money. And what you plan to do with it."

"Do with it..." Tower was fighting the urge to step out of the nearby car and take up Mark on his request to talk to the feds. "I have no idea where that money came from. Believe me on that."

"I'm putting my career on the line if I let out out of this lot."

Tower said, "When I was on the force, Lt. Smarick tried to pin the missing money from lockup on me. Even tied me to a lie detector test."

"You came back clean."

"But he always swore it was me. There was too much stink from that and I left the force."

"I know. But this is different."

"How? Smarick is still there. He'll say he was right all the time. Naw, this has to be handled my way."

"If you come in with me, I'll help speak up for your side."

"There's something brewing and I have to get my hands around it. Did you hear anything at all about a missing briefcase?"

"No. Nothing about that. Just the question about the money. Is there something I need to know about?"

"Not yet."

Tower's voice was calm and even. "What about two women?"

"No. But I need more information."

"And no murders at a bar..."

"Nothing. No murders period in the past four months. Please Frank, tell me what's going on?"

"I can't. At least not yet."

Mark David said, "I called your office, your cell and no luck. You going dark on me?"

"Let's just say I have to work in the shadows for a few days. I'll call you."

"I was going to call Shannon-"

"No, don't do that. Please stay away from her."

"Frank, is everything okay?"

Almost thirty seconds passed. Nothing. Detective Mark David looked around in the parking lot. He saw no movement. No cars. No one walking the street in front of the building.

Quiet.

He waited another two minutes but heard nothing more. He packed up the files again and went inside.

Chapter 18

Thanks to Jackie, Tower was driving a Dodge, low to the ground, with tinted windows. The thing had power, lots of room and he could sleep in the back. And it was quiet. Tower was glad he had some cash on him, went to a store and bought enough clothes to last him three days. No credit cards. He could always head back to Jackie's small house in the back if he needed. Still, he planned to live in the street, take on a new persona, no shaving, wear a hat, always keep on the sunglasses and keep his weapons ready.

He was ready to take names. First he had to make a stop.

Tower had limited experience with surveillance while on the force. That skill was increased dramatically when he moved into his own realm and did surveillance on insurance cheats. Now, he had to conduct counter surveillance on the people watching Shannon. One mistake and she could be in greater trouble.

Tower drove one block away from Shannon's home. After the affair, Tower moved into a rental apartment. Shannon stayed in the home they bought six years earlier. His best guess was she was at work. They probably watched her at her job location. However, she routinely got off work in the early afternoon since her start time was around 4a.m. Tower sat in his car, crouched down with a pair of binoculars Tray left for him in the duffle. Nearly an hour went by then he saw movement in a van parked across the street. Just a subtle movement of the van, a rocking motion meaning someone was inside and shifting weight. He jotted down the plate numbers. Later, he could call it in to Tray for a trace.

The image of Shannon being watched by strangers bothered him. He messed up the marriage and now he was responsible for putting her in line with people ready to commit murder, if needed and leave no trace of the body. His thoughts were locked on the Shannon that liked popcorn on ice cream, staying up nights watching love stories and almost always implored him to try something new. Once, she woke up at 3am. convinced him to get in the car and drive south toward Key West. No hotel room, no plans, just go. Tower ended up trying shark meat for the first time. They found a small motel near Stock Island and watched the sun go down with a glass of wine and a plate of cheese. Now, he just hoped she remembered the safe word in case there was trouble. Tower worked out something just in case trouble called. The conversation was two years ago. He took the Glock from the hiding place under the seat and placed it on the seat next to him.

Tower figured there had to be a second car. He kept scanning with the binocs until he rested on a car thirty feet from the van. A head bobbed. A third car could be on the back side of the house. He wouldn't worry about that for now.

He had to be extremely careful.

What Tower was hoping for was a shift change. The man in the car could have a pee bottle ready, so he could stay there around the clock, twenty-four hours. Still, Tower counted on a replacement. He caught a break. Twelve minutes later, another car pulled up. The car sitting there fired up the engine and got ready to leave. The new arrival slipped into the spot. The surveillance continued.

For Tower, there was a new game. He waited until the car passed him. Then he followed.

"C'mon baby," Tower whispered to the dashboard. "Lead me to your boss."

Tower kept several cars behind, taking down the plate number and driving slow. Twice the man almost lost him by driving through a yellow light. Tower kept up with him. They drove past downtown Stilton Bay, past fast-foot joints and two night clubs. Tower knew what was coming next so he slowed down. The man probably would circle his final destination at least twice to make sure he was not followed. Tower guessed right. The man stopped for a long time at Poston Street before making a left. The chances of losing him were large. Yet it was a chance he had to take. The driver circled twice then came back to Poston Street. This time, he turned right, directly into the warehouse district.

Tower followed.

The car stopped in front of a large warehouse with no name on the front. Before moving forward, the driver again seemed to be checking for others watching him. After two minutes sitting out front, he drove around to the back and parked. Tower put down the binocs and followed him, watching him walk into a side door. The place had a few windows.

Tower got out one of the toss-away phones and called Tray Colby.

"Where are you?" He asked.

Tower gave him all the directions and the exact address. He could hear Tray tapping on a keyboard, checking the place out on the computer.

"I've got the owners listed at L.M.Kreniz.Ltd." Tray read to Tower.

"I see three cars here." Tower gave Tray the tags to cars in front of Shannon's house and the one plate he could see at the warehouse.

"I'll need six minutes to work on the plates. As for the warehouse, I got nothing. No names. And the company name doesn't come up on the business listings."

"It has to be a front." Tower tried to look through the windows from his vantage point forty yards away. Nothing. "I have to get closer."

"You want me there? Backing you up?"

"Naw. I've got to do this myself. Will call you back in thirty minutes. If you don't hear from me by then, call Detective Mark David."

"You got it."

Chapter 19

Tower surveyed the area three times before making a move. Once the person was inside the warehouse, there were no signs of him. No lights. Nothing. Tower kept the Glock with him. He tracked a path in his mind and stayed with the plan. First moving to his right, Tower reached a dumpster and placed the Sig Sauer behind a wheel, as a backup. He kept going.

Moving due east of the building, he reached a tree. From here, he could check all angles of the door that had to be right around the corner. He looked up. No surveillance cameras. He stayed there a full six minutes without moving. He did not want to move too quickly. A person inside might see a flicker of shadow.

His next stop would be the side wall of the building. Tower picked a moment. He ran. His steps were quiet. He reached the wall and pressed his back against the brick. Again, he would wait. Three minutes passed. Four. Five. He moved slow against the cool bricks looking down to make sure he did not step on anything that would make noise. Tower kept going until he reached the edge of the building. He got down on the ground. A small bush gave him cover. He peered around the edge of the building. A single door was seven yards away. Closer to him was a window. He edged closer.

Tower got to the window and looked inside. The light within the warehouse was dim, yet he saw a man, his back to Tower, in front of a large chair. Around the chair were food wrappers and a glass of water. There was something else. The arms of the chair had clasps built into them to keep someone held down. The chair was empty. The man stood looking at the chair as if remembering moments of someone being trapped there. As far as Tower could see, there was no one else in the place. He looked for any paperwork, a cell phone. Nothing. The place was sparse.

In the far corner of the room there was a small bed. The man walked toward the corner, pulling of his shirt. Tower had a decision to make. He could pry open the door and get some information out of him. The guy could be a small piece of the organization. Maybe too small. If the man does not check in at a certain time, the man who called with the threats on Shannon would know immediately and she would be in trouble.

Tower thought for a moment.

He backed out of the parking lot. The place was not guarded enough to be a safe house. Where were the others? Tower took another ten minutes backtracking, picking up the Sig Sauer, then making it to the car. He placed this location in his head.
An ace to be played later. He called Tray on one of the dump phones. “A question,” Tower said.

“Whatcha need?”

“Did you pack some GPS trackers in this-”

“How long have you known me? Sure, there’s two of them in there.”

“Great. I’ve got to be in two places at the same time. I’ll plant a tracker on his car.”

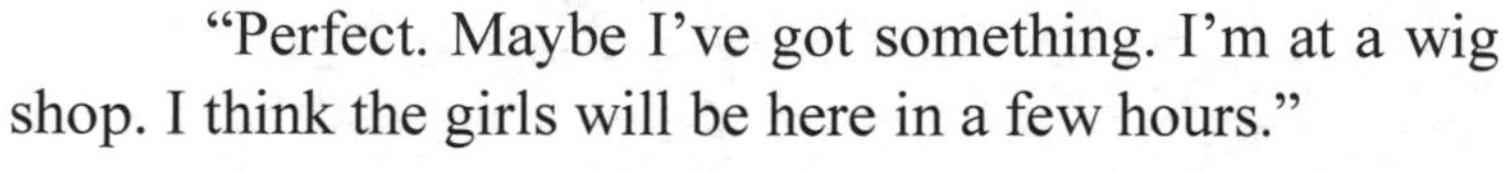

"Perfect. Maybe I've got something. I'm at a wig shop. I think the girls will be here in a few hours."

Chapter 20

Tower and Colby figured out what Ru and Wanda had planned. They must have bribed the store owner to meet them once the placed had closed for the night. An after-hours shopping spree for two women with enough money to persuade anyone to do anything.

Tower met Colby two blocks from the place, parking behind a convenience store. "We'll leave the cars here," Tower instructed. They walked the distance to the shop. Tray was ahead of Tower by several yards. When they reached the door of the place, Tray signaled for Tower to wait.

Tray stared in through the large glass panels. Then he went inside. That was not part of the plan, Tower thought. Three minutes later, Tray emerged. He was running. "Let's go?"

"What's wrong?" Tower yelled.

"They came early. They just left here." Tray huffed as he tried to get out the words as he was running. Tower joined in on the run. Once back at their cars, Tray labored to catch his breath.

"They came in. Bought twenty wigs," Tray said through taking in gulps of air. "Left him a five hundred dollar tip."

"So, where are they now?" Tower snapped on his seat belt.

"They said something about going out later tonight."

"Where?"

"Some club. He only got a partial on the name."

"Let me have it."

"Something about strip. There was a word in front of it. He thinks it starts with an L."

Tower said, "It's the Landing Strip. I know where it is. Just outside Stilton Bay." Tower checked his watch, then turned to Tray. "I've got an idea."

Chapter 21

A nervous Brent Solar studied the five story building. The place was cloaked in shadow. Most businesses would proudly light up a place, bringing attention to a name and adding security. Not here. Brent readjusted the entry pass clipped to his shirt and walked into the lobby. A check of his watch showed just passed midnight. Here, obscurity was the main goal. From the outside, the place was nondescript. There were no signs. Not even an address. There were, however, banks of surveillance cameras. Solar did his best to avoid looking into them, opting to stare at the polished marble floor. He purposely arrived a bit early, hoping to avoid contact from his co-workers.

He took the stairs instead of the elevator.

When he reached the heavy metal door outside the STREAM ROOM, he let a hiss from his lips. Another flash of another card allowed him inside. The door closed with a soft click, sealing him in the room full of computers. One more entry swipe to go. Brent placed his card to the read plate. The swipe allowed him to sign on to his computer.

He sat down. If all went well, he would tell his boss he was sick for the day. His planned two week vacation was set to start the next day, so his absence would not be noticed.

Today though was important.

Since he apparently managed to take so much information, leaving the moles in place without detection, this morning would be the test. Information that took him years to collect and steal. If any problems were detected, he wanted to be there, at his place in the cubicle, feigning anger and surprise. The IT managers would be there soon, checking the massive servers. They also had the ability to check from their home computers and laptops, looking for any breaches. Still, for Brent Solar, being in the building was the key. He figured he had until 10am. Everything was quiet.

For now.

A wrist band slid from its place under his sleeve, resting on his right hand. The man with the Eye Patch gave it to him. The band, he was told, would not be caught by the screeners in the lobby. No matter what, he was directly tied to them. They would know where he was at all times of the day. No escape. If he cut the band, they would know.

Brent slammed his hand on the desk. “Damnit,” he said to himself. The Pearls ruined everything. He spent all sleeping and waking hours figuring out the best way to kill them. The one thought that kept coming back to him: The Everglades. He would leave them tied up in the depths of the Florida Everglades, letting their legs and feet dangle in the black water, knowing alligators love to pull their prey from the banks, getting their victims locked in their jaws and spinning into a death roll in the water until they drowned. The gator could then take his time devouring them days later once they had softened up. Brent would be somewhere near to watch it go down.

Or he figured, one of the crawling monsters would creep along the grass and take them one at a time. Rock pythons, the size of a small bus, now roamed the glades, slithering for a meal.

Brent smiled.

Seconds later, the smile turned sour. He knew that if the briefcase was not found by the noon deadline, the Eye Patch man was already figuring out ways to make Brent suffer. The prospects were not good. Maybe that guy, the Frank Tower guy will come through.

Maybe. Just maybe.

"Brent!" The voice came from his left side. He looked in the direction of the sound.

"Lou, good morning," Brent said.

"I must have called you four times." Lou was now standing next to him, towering over Brent, invading his space. "You were really in a day dream or something." Lou Piscel was much bigger than Brent, standing at about six-four. He had big hands and a distinctive heavy voice. Lou turned to leave then stopped and returned to Brent's cubicle. His voice was almost a whisper.

"I'm sorry about what happened." Lou looked sincere.

Sincere, my ass, thought Brent.

Lou placed his hand on Brent's shoulder. "I just wanted you to know it was a hard decision. The other candidate was just a bit more qualified than you. You were not passed over. It was just experience. You understand, don't you?"

Brent looked down at the hand on his shoulder and wanted to rip out Lou's arm from the socket. "Sure, I understand," Brent told him. "There's other positions. And when the time comes, I'll be ready."

"I'm so glad you understand," Lou said. He removed his hand. "Thanks for being a company guy."

Lou was gone.

I've got your company guy smart-ass, Brent thought. He had known for weeks the job was going to someone else. They *did* pass him over. The move was the same for almost twenty years. Someone else got the position. The office rumors were right on target. For Brent, this latest bypass was the final factor. His motivation. The very reason for putting the plan into motion. Brent watched Lou enter his expanded office with the great view. The space was enlarged twice, with workers knocking down walls and installing chair rails and crown moulding.

Lou turned to him before closing the door and grinned.

Was he laughing? This was all funny to him. The entire office must have been in on the joke. A joke started with Lou. He turned all his anger toward his boss. Brent's jaw muscles clenched and he had to stop himself from grinding his teeth. The anger for Lou was visceral. He pointed a finger at the door with Lou's name painted in big letters.

Brent smiled again.

"I've got a surprise for you."

Chapter 22

"I don't like this." Wanda swirled her drink. "We saw a man die. We need to leave. Now."

"C'mon sweetheart, enjoy yourself. One final hunt before we move on." Ru was smiling the smile of a winner. She was wearing a new silver sparkled sequin dress, hemmed three inches shorter than when she found it on the rack. A shiny stiletto heel dangled from her right toe. "I feel good," she said. "Good night to hunt."

Wanda turned up the drink, emptying the glass, then placed it on the bar for another. She looked into a nearby mirror to admire the curls in her new wig. Her backless black dress had the plunge front she liked, letting the world see her assets. "I am black on black, in black," Wanda laughed. The drink came and she swirled the concoction until the ice stared to melt.

Danger always marked them. Once, after taking down an out-of-state tire salesman for thirty-eight grand, the two drove off on a drunken road trip. Two miles into the drive, Wanda lost control of the car and they skidded off the road into a canal. The car turned upside down. They had to claw their way out of twisted metal and shattered glass, cutting themselves in the process and swimming to shore. The money was lost.

Now Ru checked the mirror behind the counter.

One man entered the bar and sat down. They were working without their lookout person. Stan was not there to point them in the right direction for the mark. They were on their own to find a victim. Wanda looked over her left shoulder. "He looks like he doesn't have a penny." Wanda went back to her drink.

"Sweetheart, how long we gonna be here?"

"Just wait."

The one man in the place paid for his drink with a money stack resembling an amount one tossed in the charity bucket. "Naw, he's got nothing." Wanda was given the task of checking out the customers so only one person was staring across the room. "I don't think he can pay for his cab ride," she snuffed. "And he's not wearing a watch."

"We'll give it thirty minutes. Then we're off."

The ice in Wanda's drink was reduced to the size of a bean when another man walked in and sat down next to a tall speaker. The man was wearing a suit, easily going for thirteen-hundred dollars. The white shirt was unbuttoned at the top and starched to the max. He checked the time and he was wearing a diamond encrusted piece. On the left hand, he wore a gold chain. The pinky finger sported a ring and diamond the size of a cornel of corn.

"Bingo," Wanda whispered. "The guy in the corner. That's our guy. If he doesn't smile back at you in the next two minutes, we're outta here. You understand?"

"Oh, he'll smile back. I'll make sure of that." Ru swiveled toward him on the barstool. Once facing the man, she shook her long blonde locks a couple of times, letting her hair finally rest down her back. She looked down at the counter, then flashed the long fake eyelashes in the direction of the corner. He was watching her.

She smiled.

The man smiled back.

"Gotcha," she said under her breath.

Now it was Wanda's turn. She got up from her spot at the bar and walked across the room to the juke box. Her gait was slow and purposeful, her six-inch heels placed in front of her with each step like the walk of a model. The hips all fluid and moving, stretching the extra tight and very short black dress. Wanda didn't have to check. She knew every eye, including the bar tender, was staring at her every move. The new wig gave her the confidence of a woman on a mission. The Eye Patch man was a distant memory. Right now, she had the floor, she had all the attention.

She bent over.

All eyes on Wanda.

She pressed a button and in a few seconds, a hot number rocketed through the speakers, bass shaking the floor. Wanda let her hips move in time with the music. When she turned, three men were staring at her, then turned away as if they didn't want to be caught gawking too hard.

Wanda smiled.

She looked in the direction of the man in the corner and let her tongue glide over her bottom lip. She could tell he was hooked. The man didn't care if he was staring too long or too hard. Wanda sat back down at the bar and waited for another drink. Ru took her time uncrossing the legs covered with black fishnet stockings; the movement making the sequins shimmer in the bar light.

The room was theirs for the taking. All they had to do was pick the man. He would come willingly. In the corner, the possible mark ordered a drink. He pulled out a roll of one hundred dollar bills, reeled off one of them, then tucked the roll into the inside pocket of his suit coat.

Ru got the attention of the bartender. "Please tell him, we're paying for his drink."

"But he already gave me a tip," the bartender protested.

"That's okay, keep your tip. I'll give you one too. Just tell him we'll take care of his drink." Ru pulled a fifty from her tiny purse. She watched him walk to the man in the corner and got a smile of approval once the message was delivered. She looked at Wanda. "You ready?"

"Let's go."

Ru and Wanda got up and walked to the table. Wanda sat to his left. Ru took up a chair on his right, making sure if either of them spoke, he couldn't keep his attention on both of them at the same time. After initial introductions, Wanda kept talking to him. While he was distracted, Ru ran her hand over his drink.

"You've got some big hands," Ru said.

"Just lucky, I guess," the man said. Fifteen minutes into the conversation, the man wiped his brow. "Man, I think I better get to my hotel."

"Why, we can help you." Wanda was already out of her seat and standing next to him.

"Thank you. You say your name is Pearl?"

"Yes. Is your car outside?" Wanda had her arm around him. Ru was making sure there were no tabs left to be paid. She then joined Wanda at the door. The three of them walked out into the night air.

"Where is your car?" he said. "Not sure if my car is running."

"Sweetheart, we really should take your car. It will be easier later."

"No I want your car. Where is it?" He touched or attempted to reach a blue SUV. "This one, right?"

"Yes, that's it but we really need to take your car." Wanda pulled on his arm.

"Okay. Tell you what. I'm across the street at the motel. Don't need a car. Let's walk."

They crossed the street. Two women in tall heels and a man not sure of his balance. They made it to the other side of the street and he moved in the direction of 1C. He pulled out a room card and aimed the card at the door.

Wanda took the card out of his hands. "Here, let me do that for you." She opened the door to the room. There were twin beds and a suitcase on the stand, open.

The man sauntered to the bed and dropped face first. Wanda touched him. "I think he's out."

"You sure?" Ru pressed on his neck and back, then shook him. "You're right. He's out." She walked over and closed the drapes. "Okay, you know the drill. I get the watch and jewelry. You work him for the wallet. In a bit, we'll see if we can get him to talk about numbers to the safe."

They worked like a team. Wanda removed his shoes, sox and pants in less than two minutes. He was down to his underwear. She tied the ends of the pants in big knots and used the pants as a giant bag, taking out the wallet and the roll of cash and tossing them in one pants leg. Ru tossed in the nice watch and the gold chain. Neither spoke. They went about their work like precision-timed members of an elite squad. The man was worked over and trimmed down to just his shirt and underwear.

"Okay," Ru said. "Get him to talk."

Wanda got up close to him and kissed him on the cheek. "It's me. You remember me." Her voice was soothing, almost hypnotic. She rubbed his temples. Finally, he began to answer her.

"You want to share," she said. "Share with your friends. You remember the safe. What are the numbers to the safe?" She kept rubbing his temples, harder now until he was semi-awake. He mouthed words. First, she did not hear them. Wanda got him to repeat the numbers. Ru was standing nearby ready to write them down.

Numbers in hand, Ru went to the safe. She used the numbers and opened the small stash box. A single piece of paper was inside. Confused, she pulled out the paper and read it aloud to Wanda.

"All it says is look behind you."

Wanda said, "Look behind you? What does that mean?"

"That means it's over. Good to see you again ladies." Frank Tower stepped into the room.

Chapter 23

"Where have you been? We've been trying to reach you." Wanda stepped away from the man on the bed.

"Sure you were." Tower kept the Glock tucked away in the back of his pants. "Okay. You can get up now." Tower walked across the room and picked up the pants of Derreck Rock.

"I was waiting for the back rub but it never came." Rock sat up.

Wanda'a eyes widened. "You conned us."

"Seems more like you conned him," Tower said. "I see you got my note."

"Funny. Very funny." Ru was not smiling.

Derreck grabbed his pants, pulling out his money role and wallet. "Should we shoot them now?" Derreck Rock pulled up his pants.

Tower said, "He's just kidding ladies. Although the thought crossed my mind. Shannon is still in trouble. Your running out compromised her."

"We didn't mean to hurt anybody." Wanda watched Derreck deposit the money into his pocket. He noticed her staring at the roll. "This goes back into the bank."

"Thanks Derreck. Ladies, meet Derreck Rock. Private investigator. And a person who does not take drinks from strangers."

"We saw you drink." Ru looked for a place to sit. There were no chairs. "You can't prove anything."

"No?" Tower went to the small table and pulled out a tiny camera. "We've got three of these planted all around the room. All with a recording device. It's all on tape."

"But we saw you take the drink." Ru pressed for an answer.

Derreck said, "You saw me take the drink up to my mouth. I never swallowed. When you weren't looking, I poured the drink on the carpet."

Ru slipped the purse onto her shoulder. "So what now? The police?"

Tower checked his friend. "All in due time. The police will know everything soon. Right now, what I really want is the briefcase. Where is it?"

Wanda looked at Ru with a stare. "I told you I didn't like this. We shoulda been out of here."

"The briefcase!" Tower had lost his patience.

"We have it stashed away." Ru pointed a weak finger in the direction of Stilton Bay.

"And the money?"

"It's all there. We just spent a few thousand. That's it. Bought a car. Clothes." Ru looked down at the gleaming dress and shoes. "Can't run in these."

"We're going to get the briefcase." Tower checked his watch. 2:47a.m. "Let's go."

Another person entered the room. Tray Colby rushed in carrying a laptop. He looked anxious. "You know our friend?" he asked Tower.

Frank Tower took the laptop. The screen showed movement of the GPS signal he placed on the car at the warehouse. “You’re right.”

“You can check it. He’s on the move.”

Chapter 24

Lou Piscel left work early. With a midnight start time, leaving work at 5a.m. meant his neighborhood was still in a pre-dawn darkness. He stepped from the car and was bathed in the light of a near full moon. He picked this area because it was far from the hustle of downtown. Here, the only noise came from birds and an occasional lizard scampering through dried leaves. During his regular routine, he always checked his mail a day later, in the morning after his shift ended.

He was expecting a response from his daughter Elaine. She moved out three years ago, dropped out of college and traveled Europe spending the money he had sent her for studying. The phone conversations did not go well. Not for the father who expected Cum Laude for the return on his money. Not for the father who worked up to twelve hours a day so his daughter would have plenty of spending money so she could use all her time becoming the next corporate lawyer or hedge fund manager. Wasting her time in Europe was not what he expected. Lou finally managed to forgive her. After all, this was his only child.

He put everything into the letter and now he was confident she would come around. Go back to college. Make him the proud father.

Lou stepped from the car and noticed the early morning sky and the display of stars next to the moon. He liked this time of the morning. Quiet time.

PEARLS

Four large windows made up the front of the house. When Lou arrived home, he always stood on the sidewalk and looked through the windows for any movement. He kept a light on near the kitchen, giving him a reference. Anyone moving in front of the light would be seen from the outside. He prided himself on being able to check the grounds easily once he was out of the car.

On this morning, he forgot to leave on the porch light. The front door was streaked in shadow.

He put his hand on the metal mailbox, one designed to look like a house similar to his one story home on Dressdon Lane. Inside the tiny wooden house, there was a metal box for the mail. Lou started to pull down the lid.

He dropped his keys and had to search for them in the dark. Lou cursed at himself for being clumsy. The keys must have fallen in the grass. He kicked at the two-inch tall blades and stomped the ground in search of the house keys. For a moment he thought about where he placed the flash light in his car. That too, would be a search. On the tenth kick in the grass, he heard the clink of metal. He found the keys. Lou stuck the key ring in his pocket rather than take the chance of dropping them again. He again stood in front of the mailbox and rested his hand on the lid.

He pulled the lid down.

The blast ripped through him, making his organs, face, ribs and upper body all part of the hot spray of blood and tissue rocketing in the direction of the home across the street. The roadway was littered with paper and remnants of the bomb. The four-foot tall mail box was reduced to a blackened area of burned grass. A smoke cloud formed above the houses and bits of bomb material, bone fragments and blood rained down on the street. Lights went on in houses all down the block. All of the windows in Lou's house were reduced to shattered glass and metal. The concussion waves caused car alarms to sound as far as three blocks away. Windows in a nearby house were smashed. A piece of femur bone stuck in the wall. The mist and smell of exploded bomb fragments hung in the air. Within two minutes sirens could be heard. The first few people came out of their homes coughing, others covered their ears, still ringing from the loud noise.

In front of the mail box the only thing remaining for investigators was a pair of shoes, still smoking from all the heat.

Chapter 25

"You think someone is following you?" Jackie studied the woman standing in the lobby of the Never Too Late Rehabilitation Center.

"I *know* someone is following me." Shannon Tower was patting her right foot. She stepped into the room turning once in the direction of the street. Her hair was out of place, the eyes tired, her shoes didn't match the outfit. "I've been calling Frank. I can't reach him at the office, his cell phone goes right to voicemail. No one has heard from him. So, where is he?"

"I don't know. He must be working on something." Jackie checked the time. 6a.m. "It's really early."

"And what is his car doing out back?" Shannon looked past Jackie as if looking for him in the arrangement of rooms set aside for patients.

"Well, he's not here. I haven't talked to him." Jackie tried to show concern.

"I know we're not seeing each other right now and I told him to stay away but I really need him." Shannon used her hands to press her hair into place. "When he was on the force and even now in his PI work, he always stayed in touch. I understand there are investigations and he can't say much, but he always let me know where he was. Now I can't find him."

"How do you know you're being followed?"

Shannon turned and peeked through the window. “I know they’re out there. They think I can’t see them but they’re there. They’re at my house. Frank taught me a lot of things and I know when someone is watching me.”

“You go to the police?”

“Not yet. I don’t want to mess up something Frank might be doing. Please, I know he told you something. Where is he?”

Ten seconds became twenty. Then thirty. Jackie was breaking down under the pressure. She kept a promise to Frank. “I really shouldn’t say anything.”

Shannon moved closer to Jackie, putting an arm around her. “I have to know something. Please. Anything. Was he here? I mean, why else would his car be here?”

“Yes. He was here. Stayed here for a day. Then he left.”

“Where did he go?”

“That, I don’t know. I really don’t. He stayed and left.”

“Was he with anyone? I mean I tried calling Tray. Nothing.”

“Well...”

“Well? What does that mean? Was he with someone?”

“Yes. He was with someone. You’re right Shannon, maybe we don’t want to get involved.”

“Who was he with?” More of a demand than a question. Her shoulders sagged as if in anticipation of something bad.

“I really don’t want to say.”

Shannon let her arm drop and got in Jackie’s face.

"Who was there when you needed someone to bail you out of jail? What was it? Five years ago..."

"You were."

"And you made a promise to me, when I posted that bail, didn't you?"

"This is different."

Shannon's foot was patting again. "Different? I'm calling in my favor. I put up bail for you more than once and didn't tell Frank. You turned your life around. Stopped doing crack. I was always there for you. Now be there for me. Who was Frank with? I need an answer now."

Jackie hesitated, then, "He was with two women."

"Two women? What two women?" Shannon's voice had a hard edge. Her voice was so loud, two people opened their doors and looked into the hallway. Jackie turned to them. "Go back to bed. Please, go back to bed. Everything is okay."

But everything was not okay. Shannon had an image of Frank with two women staying in the back house. She knew all about the back house. A mistress and all the lies kept her from fully trusting Frank again. Months after the affair was over, Frank pleaded with her to try again. Don't destroy the marriage. Shannon was just coming around to the idea of giving him a set of the new keys she had made. Just about ready to open her life to Frank Tower one more time. She trusted him again just like when they got married. And now this.

Shannon's eyes were blazing brown. Her arms were stacked tight against her chest. She hissed the words, "two women."

"I really don't know that much about them."

"What did they look like?"

"Well..."

"Jackie..."

"They looked like professionals."

"Professional what?"

"Call girls."

"What!"

Shannon walked in a small circle, her feet stomping the worn tile with each step. "I stayed up all night worried about him and he's here with two hookers."

"Please Shannon, I think it was business. They were his clients."

"So now he's representing hookers. I didn't know they had insurance problems."

"Shannon-"

"He's weak," Shannon words blasted off the walls. "Legs and boobs and he's over the edge."

Jackie matched Shannon's steps, grabbed her by the shoulders and sat her down in a chair. "Listen to me. In the short time Frank was here, I got the impression these women were in trouble. At first I thought the first thing you did. You have to give Frank a chance. I really believe he is trying to help them. Think about it, if someone is following you, then it has something to do with these women. More than anything, Frank needs you right now. He'll get in touch with you. What you have to do is be ready for some kind of signal."

"What about the police?"

"He never told me about contacting PD. You know I don't get along with them anyway. What he told me was some people might come by and the less I knew the better. What I think is, you are in trouble. For now, If you don't mind, why don't you stay with me."

Shannon thought about what Jackie said. "Maybe you're right. I've got to follow along with this." Shannon got up, relief in her eyes. "I'm going home and wait for him."

When she reached the door, Jackie caught her with a question. "I know he messed things up, but you still love him, don't you?"

Chapter 26

Donald Crespo surveyed the block and he still did not like the set-up. Four teams of K-9 bomb sniffing dogs moved from house to house, yet as far as he could tell, seventeen homes needed to be evacuated.

Now.

Growing up, Crespo did not like puzzles. His grandmother always sent them at Christmas and he felt the wrapped package, trying to figure out the ones, for sure, were puzzles and shoved to the back of the tree. A few times he guessed wrong and found out late in the morning she had actually sent very nice games. He was too impatient back then. A trait he learned to dismiss as the head of the Stilton Bay bomb squad.

"Get those people moving." Crespo shouted to two uniforms. "We don't know if there's a second bomb."

Donald Crespo was facing a puzzle. A puzzle of burnt wood, bomb fragments, body parts and human spray. And all of it now in minute pieces so small, only an expert could tell them all apart. He stared at the task. The mail boxes of thirty-seven homes were inspected. Another fourteen still needed a check by the dogs. A seven block radius around the bomb center was being evacuated. Each house also needed a sweep. All that would take time. Crespo was worried. He did not know if the bomber had another device in place. The shoes found at the original scene told him there was one victim.

On his left, Detective Mark David approached. "I'm the next one up," David said. "This is my case. I'll stay clear and let you do your work but do you have a sense on when my team can get in there?"

"Give me an hour. That should do it." Crespo never faced Mark David. His attention was on the mobile robot, making sure it was ready in case they found another bomb. Crespo finally turned to Mark David. "From the witnesses who were here, they talked about white smoke. That's important because now I know, mostly likely the type of blast they used." Crespo took his arm and waved at the expanse of crime tape and now empty streets. "We got a lot of homes to check. I don't know if this person used a microswitch, mercury, was it set off by radio? By mobile phone on the other side of the world." He wiped the sweat off his brow. "Or even by pager."

Mark David stepped back and walked to his car, content to wait it out.

Crespo studied the debris field and the blast pattern blooming out from where the mail box once stood. A uniform walked up to him, letting him know every home was now empty. A half-block down the street, he got a hand signal from the K-9 teams. The inspection of the homes was finished.

All clear.

Crespo walked with a calm assurance of someone who spent two tours in Iraq. Another in Afghanistan. He knew his bombs. The sun glinted off something in the blocked street. Before he moved in, Crespo took out his camera. He spent the next fifty minutes photographing everything, from every angle. When he thought he was done taking photographs, he shot sixty more. He took small samples of material off the wall of the house across the street. Soon he had filled eighty small packets with evidence. The key, he thought, was to take his time. Put the puzzle back together in his mind.

He studied the smashed windows of the car in the driveway. Crespo walked toward the shiny piece of metal on the ground and smiled.

He took a clasp and picked it up, examining the find very closely. Crespo walked the piece over to his truck. Once inside, he turned on his equipment. The metal fragment was placed in the slot. When the job was done several minutes later, he turned in the direction of Detective Mark David and yelled.

"There's something you have to see. Now."

Chapter 27

"You sure about this?" Mark David pulled out a writing pad.

"Well, there's not enough points to stand up in court but there's enough for me to say this is the fingerprint of a Brent Solar."

"And how do you know that?"

"There was a small print left on what I believe is the pressure plate made to make the thing go off."

Detective Mark David was writing so hard, he could be heard several feet away. He stopped. "Explain this to me again?"

Crespo stared at the driveway. "The way I see it, the bomber set up the device in the mailbox. When the mail carrier dropped off the letter, the pressure plate connection was made. The thing was crafted so that the next person who opened the mailbox, got the surprise."

"But that could have been the mail carrier, the next day." Mark David shared in the direction of the box.

"Sure. It could have been the mailman, a neighbor stealing the mail, a person stuffing an ad, anyone. The next person was going to die. The killer was just taking a chance it would be the mark. And by he way, we think your dead man is Lou Visceral."

Mark David didn't even blink. "Yes, we have a rundown on him. He left work and got home early in the morning. We figured he approached the box."

Crespo said, “At first, we didn’t get any hits on the print. We opened up the search to all people who have to register their fingerprints and bingo.”

Mark David studied the small fragment of metal. “And you know who worked for Piscel? Brent Solar.”

Chapter 28

Brent Solar had never tasted his own blood. All that changed.

"Get him up." The man with the Eye Patch circled around Brent Solar as if trying to figure out what part of his body should be attacked next.

Brent Solar used his tongue to care for a cut lip. His entire body was still stinging from the dozens of punches landed on his face and upper body. His hands were tied behind him and he could not attend to the rings of pain ringing across his chest and arms. The wristband was cutting into his hand.

"You don't understand-"

The taller one with the small scar on his face didn't let Solar finish. A fist crashed into his jaw so hard the tall man shook his fist from the impact. Brent Solar felt himself ready to drift into unconsciousness. Eye Patch man grabbed Brent's face. "Oh no you don't. Don't go to sleep on me just yet. We're just half way done."

In the background, a flatscreen television was blasting. A news anchor was reporting on the bomb blast and a neighborhood in chaos.

Solar was sure both his eyes were swollen. Sweat and blood settled into his eyes, making them sting. More sweat trickled down from his forehead. He just wanted to sleep.

Eye Patch made sure that did not happen. "I've spent years putting this together, making sure every move was quiet. The people we killed were never found. We clean up. Everything put back just the way it was, like we were never there. Everything to keep this quiet. Now, you come along and make it all public."

"They don't know anything." Solar squinted at the television. "All they know is there was a bomb."

Eye Patch walked while he talked. "They will know who that man is who was blown up. They will know you worked for him. They will know everything you did in the past few years. Everything. They will investigate the projects you worked on. Check and double-check your computer habits. And when they are done, they will know about me."

"No." Solar spoke and blood seeped into his mouth. The metallic taste almost made him cough. "They don't know anything. I was careful. You don't understand."

"I understand everything."

Solar coughed. "This man made my life miserable."

"You couldn't wait." Eye Patch was within inches of Solar's face. "You couldn't wait until this operation was over. You had all that money. Just like you couldn't wait with those two women. And still no briefcase. You are a walking mistake."

Solar's head drooped. "Just kill me now," he said.

"We have to hope Mr. Tower delivers. We have a few ways to find them ourselves but I prefer to stay out of the picture."

Solar looked up. "I didn't think."

"Just think about this. All we need to keep around is your eye and a finger. The rest of you can be a memory."

Chapter 29

"Okay, the place is yours. It's clear. No booby-traps." Don Crespo walked out of apartment 3C pulling off his helmet and gear.

Brent Solar's apartment.

Six members of the bomb squad started to pack up. One would remain. Crespo and four of the team would return to the Piscel home and continue with the investigation.

Detective Mark David snapped on his gloves and stepped into 3C. The place was a two bedroom, two bath unit on the third floor with a view of the parking lot and no balcony. A clean countertop matched the outside of the fridge. No stickies. He studied the floor. Not even a crumb on the dark-grained wood planks. Crime techs would come next, swiping the surfaces of everything for bomb making material and DNA.

By the time the bomb squad was finished, Mark David had his search warrant.

Brent Solar didn't leave much in the way of his intentions. The detective checked the bathroom, the tub, toilet, closets and even pulled apart six baseboards. Nothing. There were no notes. No work table where he would have assembled the bomb. Solar was indeed careful.

And no computer.

An hour into the search, Mark David turned the place over to the crime techs. Let them find a lead. The next stop for the detective would be the business where Solar worked but there was a problem. Two lawyers served him with a protection order saying he could not have access to the building.

Mark David thought about two things: who had the power to impede a homicide investigation. And the last question from Tower, if he was working any homicides.

Chapter 30

The man with the scar walked to the far side of the room and raised his gun to the temple of a sleeping Brent Solar. “You want me to do him now?”

Response from the Eye Patch was quick. “No. Let him sleep. What you’re doing is too quick. I want him awake when we kill him. I want him to see it coming.” He turned off the television. “Up to now we have built everything on being in the shadows. After what he did, we have no choice. We have to speed things up. We have a very limited time or this whole project will fail.

Shannon Tower circled her house twice before parking. She did not see anyone following her but her feelings never let her down before. *And where was Frank?*

She walked into the house searching, not even sure what she was looking for or what she would find. Shannon checked the doors to see if there was any tampering. She checked closets and under the bed. Maybe she was over-reacting.

She had been on vacation and it was about to come to an end soon. Shannon thought about leaving town but decided to lounge, visit the beach and take in a movie. The entire time she watched her phone. No call from Frank. If he was going to try and make up for things, this was the perfect time, she thought.

Like a vacated building coming down in a demolition explosion, Shannon's trust for Tower crashed into a heap the day she found out he was cheating on her with a client. Rebuilding that trust would take time. A lot of time. Tower tried to explain it away and later, facts showed the woman in question had a pre-determined plan to seduce Tower in order to pry facts from him in the murder of her friend's family. Shannon reasoned Tower would never have given her information unless he fell to the base fault of any man: temptation of sex.

And then the mistress was murdered.

Tower solved the case and all suspicion of Tower was erased but the residual impact on Shannon was still there. She stared at the wall where once dozens of pictures of them adorned every corner of every room.

Her thoughts kept going back to Jackie's description of two slinky women with Tower. Two reasons for him to slip. She kept thinking about what he was doing with them. And why was he out of touch. This was difficult, she thought, when all your trust for Tower could fit into a walnut shell. Still, the most disturbing fact kept tearing at her core. Why did she care? Let him go. Move on. She knew the reason and she didn't like what she was thinking. There was still a spark. A reason to love him.

For now, she was locked into Tower and could not move on to another man.

"Where are you," she said to the empty house. Shannon could not hide it, she missed him. With no word, he could be in trouble, and maybe the trouble extend to her as well. She glanced again at her phone. No message.

Shannon parted the windows and thought she saw movement in the back yard. She stared for a long time, and watched the sun give nurturing radiance to the elephant ear plants in her garden. Maybe it was nothing.

Chapter 31

"Okay, this is how we're going to do this," Tower stood near the door. The place was packed with five adults in the cramped motel room quarters. "Derreck, you're done."

Derreck was packing up the recording gear. "But the fun is just beginning."

"Not for you. You're outta here. Tray, get the car ready. Ladies, we're all traveling together. We're going to get the briefcase. Someone's life depends on this."

Ru spoke first. "We left it with our fence."

"He has a locker. He doesn't know what's in it. We told him it was clothes." Wanda kept her finger in a curl of her wig.

"We're on the move. Let's go."

All five made it down the stairs. Tower kept waiting for the two to run but they'd have to take off their heels first.

Fully dressed, Derreck Rock got into his car and drove off. Tower waved a hand of thanks. "Wanda, you ride up front with Tray. Ru, you're in the back with me."

She smiled. "Anything you say, sweetheart."

Tower watched them close. They got into the car without any protests. Tray studied his laptop. "Yep. Not sure where he's going but the car is moving."

For a quick second, Tower glanced at the laptop. He saw the same tracking movement Colby recognized. The subject at the warehouse was in the car, moving.

"Let's go." Tower kept his Glock visible. He pulled out a burner phone and kept the device close to him, away from the eyes of his passengers. Tower typed in just one word. He sent the message on its way. Thirty seconds later, Tower rolled down the window and tossed the phone out the window. A look of concern etched on his face.

Once they were inside the city limits of Stilton Bay, Tray turned down Fepson street, making a left at Jewel Boulevard. "Is your fence expecting you back? Or will this be a surprise?" Tower looked forward through the windshield.

"We have a key." Wanda pulled it from the purse then shoved the key back inside.

Tower looked at Ru and Wanda. "If they are coming to the bar searching for you two, they'll ask a few questions and head back to Stilton Bay. Hopefully, we've got some time on them."

Ten minutes into the ride, Tower again turned to Ru. "Why did you leave the house and run off?"

"Because we were putting too much heat on you and your wife. We had to get away. We just stayed too long."

"You got that right," Wanda yelled.

"Pull over." Tower ordered Colby to drive to the side of the road.

"You sure Frank?"

"Pull over. Now."

Colby slowed down and let the car drift quietly to the road shoulder. And stopped. He turned around with a certain curiosity, met the ragged look in Tower's eyes, then turned quickly back to the front. Tower got out first, walking fifteen feet in front of the car, motioning to Ru and Wanda to meet him in the bright columns of light coming from the front car beams. Off in the distance, Tower heard crickets and the sounds coming out of the thickets of Brazilian pepper tree. The hard clank of heels on the roadway echoed each time they took a step toward him.

Frank stared at them. "Don't run off again. Not unless you give me some warning. That okay?"

Both Ru and Wanda nodded.

"Any idea what this is about? What these guys are up to?"

Wanda lifted her foot for only a moment, as though something on the ground was about to bite off her foot. "We're trying to figure that out. We have no idea. They only seem interested in the briefcase."

"And you left it behind?" Tower was shaking his head.

"Sweetheart, we weren't going to take that thing with us. Who knows what's in it."

Tower studied the two of them. The car lights gave a clear outline of their hip curves and legs, giving the appearance they were on stage. Wanda's exposed toes in the tall heels were the same color as her tight-to-the-skin dress. Her cleavage line changed as she talked with an animated way of reinforcing her words. Ru's bright eyes shone, even in the dim light. For a moment, for just a second, he felt himself falling to the allure of two beautiful women. Thoughts of being pulled in by his past mistress consumed him. Like the sirens of Greek mythology, Tower could imagine himself being seduced and conquered by the two in front of him. Time to go, he thought.

"And you two had no idea about this briefcase before you met him?"

Wanda pulled on her wig. "No. Nothing. No idea. Can't say it any clearer."

Wanda took a step toward the car. "We're not going to cover this up. We wanted his money. Plain and simple. If you're not supposed to hear about our crimes and you're a PI, too bad. We planned to take his money, have a great time and move on to the next mark. Only we didn't expect all this. That damn briefcase is getting people killed."

The fence had a location that was a pawn shop connected to a duplex. This, Tower figured, was where Ru and Wanda could crash until they left town. The shop had a front section that was open to customers with a front door key. The key worked for both the door and the individual lockers. Wanda worked the key quietly. The sun was just about to come up.

Once inside, Tower watched closely. Wanda went directly to a locker, inserted the key and pulled out the duffle and the briefcase. She kept the duffle and handed the case to Tower.

"Thanks."

"You have to let us change clothes. It won't take long." Wanda dabbed at the corner of her wig.

"Make it quick." Tower examined the briefcase.

All four walked outside the pawn shop entrance, to a darkened short sidewalk leading to the side apartment. Usually, Tower would give a woman plenty of space and back-off while they changed outfits. Not this time. Before he let them into the room, Tower checked for a window in the bathroom. Any escape. No window. Once he was satisfied everything was clear, he let them in the room. Tower stood inside the door.

Tray stayed outside as a lookout.

"You want to watch?" Ru smiled and spoke over her shoulder. "You can, if you want."

"I just have to keep you two in sight."

"No problem." Ru dropped the silver outfit with the flick of her hand, sliding a strap and letting the dress drop to the floor. Tower looked away. "You can keep watching, sweetheart." She moved her body in a way so Tower had to see her. Ru was proud of her angular legs and hips. She took her time, giving Tower a full show.

He kept turning away from her.

Wanda stood behind an opened closet door. She tossed the black dress in the corner. Both of them pulled out jeans and stretched them over legs and toes. Low heels came next. "See there, done." Ru smacked her flat stomach.

Tower opened the door. Tray was standing there. He had a weird look on his face as if someone just stole his life's savings. "Sorry Frank. I didn't see him coming."

Tray walked into the room with a gun jammed against his head. A man with a torn shirt, and bleach-streaked jeans followed. “No one is going anywhere,” he shouted.

Tower said, “Who is this?”

Wanda offered the answer. “Our fence.”

Chapter 32

"How did?-" Tower answered his own question. "The surveillance cameras."

"Yep. Got seven of 'em." The smile revealed a set of gray-green teeth. There was a gap to the right where one tooth was missing. Tower guessed the man was about five-foot-seven, right-handed by his gun use, slight build, around one-hundred-fifty pounds, and graying just slightly at the temples.

"Stringer, you don't need to do this." Wanda moved from her spot by the closet and was walking toward him. The gun barrel moved from Tray's head to Wanda's midsection.

"Yeah, I got to do this. Just stay right where you are."

His nickname described him perfectly. Stringer had long thin arms, spotted with unreadable tattoos. His hair was a matted mess of strands dangling down to his shoulders. He wore his shirt half out of his pants and his right shoelace was untied. Everything he had on dangled off him as if two sizes too large. The biggest thing on his body was the gun he aimed at them.

For Tower, everything was timing. First, they had stayed too long and the decision to let them get changed was a bad one. He figured Stringer probably saw them drive in, saw them enter the pawn shop on his seven cameras and then saw the briefcase. He also probably had the place rigged for audio and heard the whole thing.

Still, Tower tried to figure out if he had enough time to get his Glock before Stringer pulled the trigger. He dismissed the idea for the moment.

"Listen to her, Stringer." Tower moved a bit to his right, to widen the spaces between the subjects in the room, making it tougher for him to see all four people in one glance. Make him turn his head.

"Don't move." Stringer again put the gun to the head of Tray.

Tower tried to reason. "You're not part of this. If you put the gun down right now, we all walk away. Nothing said. It's over."

"You gonna pay me, like the other guy?" Stringer rolled his tongue over the worn teeth.

"The other guy?" Bad things moved through Tower's thoughts. "Did you see this guy? Is he wearing a patch?"

"That's the man. Came to see me. Already gave me a handful of money. More to come, he said, when he gets here."

Bad things confirmed. Tower knew they didn't have much time. "You don't understand. That man isn't going to give you any more money. He's going to kill you, along with the rest of us."

"Mister, I haven't seen that much money in my life. I am set. When that guy gets here, you're all his."

"Listen to me. The man wants something from us. Once he gets it, he will kill everyone connected to us. We'll all die. Is that clear?"

"I don't believe you."

Ru said, "Listen to him. How long have you known us? We've done a lot of deals. We always trusted you. Now trust us. We saw the man with the patch kill our friend. Stan tried to work him. Now he's dead. Think about it."

For a flash, Tower saw the micro wheels in his head turning. Money or stay alive. Tower knew the deal. Stringer thought he could beat the odds and get both. Tray looked over to Tower. A signal?

Stringer had the point position and Tower cursed himself for not being in the right place. He was a former cop and he walked away from the front door, the only place of entrance and escape. When he walked away, he gave up control of the space, even with his Glock. Stringer was in the doorway now, with a weapon, with a hostage and a room full of bystanders, including himself. *Damnit.*

Tower looked past the searching eyes of Tray. Car lights were moving into place in the parking lot. Eye Patch was here. Tower knew he was running out of time. Soon, the margin of getting out alive would be even smaller. Three more guns in the room would do that unless he could come up with something.

The entire room must have heard the same thing. Foot steps coming toward them. Heavy steps. Two thugs, both well over six-feet tall, stepped into the room. Tower sized them up to be holding .22 calibre hand guns with mounted suppressors. And both carried a second weapon in their waist. One man, the one on the right when he entered the room, had a very small cut on his left cheek. The cut was healed and appeared to be a wound from years prior. Neither one said anything. The man on the left wore a small ring on his pinky. Both looked toward the door.

Eye Patch entered. “Let’s get this over with.” He turned to Stringer. “Thank you for calling me. I will increase the amount I first told you.”

Stringer smiled the smile of a dentist’s nightmare. “Thank you.”

Eye Patch nodded to one of his men. “My man here will take over. Everyone please move to the back of the room.” When he gave the command to move, Stringer noticed he was included in the order. “Me too? I’ve been holding them for you.”

“Yes. And we thank you for that.” Eye Patch sounded congenial. “Just give us your weapon and we’ll make all the adjustments.”

“You hear that? You’re part of the adjustments.” Tower still had his Glock tucked away. By his last count, there were more than seven weapons in the room. Tower still needed to be frisked, unless they were planning to just shoot him where he stood, weapon in his jeans.

Eye Patch lowered his voice to a calm tone. “Come now, Stringer. We have plans for you. Don’t forget we couldn’t do anything without your help.” He turned to Tower. “You were supposed to make yourself known to me immediately once you got the briefcase. Planning to contact the authorities, Mr. Tower?”

“The authorities, as you call them, are looking for me. You have anything to do with the money getting into my account?”

"I heard about that. Pity you won't be around to spend it. The government, I am sure, is watching it and they will continue to watch it when we yank it back."

"You have that kind of power?"

Eye Patch grinned. "You have no idea." He moved away from the doorway.

Tower didn't want to convey his intentions and tried not to let his eyes wander toward the open space. The point of control was unoccupied. No one was in the doorway.

Timing.

There were only so many seconds before Eye Patch would demand the following: the removal of Tower's gun and for Stringer to hand over his weapon. The question was which one would come first. The biggest threat before Eye Patch was Tower and his Glock. He would be a priority.

Unless Stringer made this an issue.

Tower said, "Go ahead Stringer, give him your gun. Trust the man."

"Shut up Tower." For Eye Patch, it seemed, things were wearing thin.

There was just one light on in the room. Even though the sun was coming in, with all the windows covered in a small, dank duplex, the place could be dark in a hurry.

Stringer said, "I think I better leave and let you have these people. If one of your men could give me my money, I'll be going-"

The bullet hit Stringer before he could finish his sentence. We just heard the burp of the silencer. A plume of red saturated his chest. The first shot was quickly followed by a second, this time hitting the fence operator and part-time pawn shop owner in the forehead, just above the nose. He dropped like a man falling without purpose, without a reason for his death. The look of surprise was still on Stinger's face when Tray took his fist and smashed the light bulb.

Tower ran to the door and slammed it closed, leaving the room in near darkness. By memory, he knew where everyone was in the room. His Glock was out of his waistband before he took another breath and fired off two rounds in the direction of where Eye Patch and his two men were standing. The explosion of the Glock covered up any sounds of the suppressors. Tower hoped Tray was on the ground reaching for Stringer's gun.

He heard Ru and Wanda's screams since the first bullet hit Stringer. They were still yelling. Tower felt and heard steps coming his way. The same heavy steps he heard in the parking lot. Before he fired, a punch caught him in the right jaw sending him crashing against the door. He rolled on the ground and felt the carpet fibers ripping against his face.

He got back up on his feet. This time Tower yanked the heavy covering off one window, letting in a bit of sunshine. The sudden blast of light showed on the face of one of the men. The man with the scar on his cheek was wounded. He opened the door with a quick motion and was gone. The second man was on the ground, next to Stringer.

Dead.

Wanda and Ru were huddled in the closet, eyes widened and hands up against their faces. Tray was up against the wall checking to see if he had any injuries. He was not hurt.

Tower looked around for Stringer's gun. Nothing. Next, Tower searched the room for the briefcase. Tray pointed to the bed. He reached under the mattress and pulled out the briefcase. The duffle bag was in the closet with Ru and Wanda.

A look of relief moved into their faces. The light from the sun was darkened by shadow. Someone was standing in the doorway. Tower turned and found himself staring face to face with a man holding a gun.

Brent Solar stepped into the room.

Chapter 33

"Nice to see you again." Brent Solar was not smiling. His attention was focused on the briefcase. Before Tower had a chance to move toward the door, Eye Patch was behind Solar, a gun pointed to his head. Behind Eye Patch was another man, one Tower recognized from the warehouse. Instead of staring at him through binoculars, Tower saw him as about six-foot-six, more than two hundred pounds, hands rough, like a boxer, with a square head, almost the width and shape of Frankenstein. He also had a .22 loaded with a silencer. The gun was pointed directly at Ru and Wanda.

Eye Patch said, "The games are over. Mr. Tower, the choice is yours. You have five seconds to drop your weapon or the first two shots will be your friends in the closet."

Tower let the Glock fall to the carpet, just inches from the growing pool of blood near Stringer's head.

Eye Patch smiled. "Good." He nodded in the direction of Solar. The man moved fast, stepping around the body on the floor, pulling the briefcase from Ru, running his fingers over the hinges.

"Can't wait to show you what I can do." Brent Solar smiled the smile of a man about to do harm. Tower sized up the room but he didn't have many options. "The police will be here. I'm sure someone heard something."

“We’re leaving.” Eye Patch looked down at the sprawling body of Stringer. “Our people will be here to clean things up. No need for the police to find him.”

With a wave of his gun and from the warehouse man, Eye Patch and three guns trained on Tower, motioning them to leave. They followed his instructions and walked to a waiting van. The warehouse man adjusted flex cuffs on all four of them and put restraints on Tower’s ankles.

Eye Patch inspected the work. “Not bad. You’re all going with us.” Before slamming the van door shut, he turned to Tower. “And for being a bad boy, I’m afraid your precious Shannon will have to suffer.”

Chapter 34

His hair was long gone years ago, then he cut it short for all the para-military work in the jungle. The stuff never grew back. As far as Bald Man could remember, there were seventeen kills, four villages burned to the ground and he had survived two helicopter crashes. Someone, he reasoned, was on his side. More than anything, he wanted to spit. He held it in. Opening the window might mean giving his target some kind of warning and he didn't want to do that. Not right now. He was still pissed. Rather than being in the front of the operation, he was stuck watching the house of someone named Shannon.

His cell vibrated against his side. He picked up the phone. The message was quick and one-sided. He never said a word, only listened. Once the conversation was over, he put the phone down and went into another mode: give pain and suffering. Bald Man pulled a knife from under his car seat. The .22, with silencer was tucked into his pants where he had sewn a holster. He smiled at the brilliance of the thing. The gun was in his pants and out of the way from staring eyes.

Inside his right pocket was a handkerchief, soaked with the smelling ingredients to put a rhino to sleep. He now liked his assignment. He could do anything he wanted to her, take his time, get to know her, make her do things to him, then put an end to everything. His smile was erased as soon as he left the car. He was alone but he didn't mind. No need for anyone else. He had faced the bravest forest fighters, going for days without water or making any movement, waiting to strike at the precise moment. For Shannon, his target, the moment was now.

No need to take her anywhere, he could do the deeds right there in the house. Before he left the car, he had checked his laptop one last time. He was watching her. She was sitting in the bedroom, near the patio door. His breathing started to pick up, anticipating the greeting he was going to give her. For days, he thought about the surprised look on her face when his hand would cover her nose and mouth with the cloth. Bald Man walked calmly up to the door as though he owned the place. Once there, he leaned his head on the door and listened. In his packet, he was sent a key to get inside. He eased the key in the lock. There were two quick looks down the street to make sure no one was watching.

Everything was set.

He turned the knob and went inside.

Chapter 35

Even with the blindfold on, Tower tried to remember the left and right turns. He remembered the feel of the roads, how certain sections of the county felt as a passenger or driver, the pick-up in speed if they moved to the expressway. Maybe he could determine where they were going. He turned to his right, only to get a hard hit across the head.

"No movement." The voice belonged to Eye Patch.

Tower's thoughts turned to Shannon. All of his attempts to stop the men in the van, chasing down the Pearls, it was all meant to protect Shannon. Was he too late?

"The world is going to come down on you if you do anything to us." Tray Colby's voice was missing the conviction behind his words.

"Ah, Mr. Colby. Isn't that your name? I'm glad you spoke. Reminded me something I need to do." Eye Patch moved around in his seat. Tower could hear him moving around in his seat on the right side of the van. The next thing he heard was a loud smack of metal or some instrument against flesh. Both Ru and Wanda screamed. They're yelling told Tower one thing; it was Colby getting hit. He heard another crack of a weapon against skin, then a grunt.

"Stop it," Tower yelled.

"My, my, my, Mr. Tower. You seem to be concerned. Did something happen? That's right, you can't see anything. Remove his blindfold. For just a second. I want you to see what you caused."

Hands and fingers carefully moved the blindfold down from Tower's eyes. Across the seat, to his right, Colby was slumped over in his seat, still blindfolded with blood streaming down from his forehead. His breathing was shallow and he needed medical attention.

"Pull over. He needs help." Tower tried to move toward Colby.

Eye Patch said, "Don't move, Mr. Tower. If you do, the next thing that will happen is we put two rounds behind his left ear. Do you want that, Mr. Tower?"

Tower sat back in his seat.

"Where are you taking us?" Tower took the moments of being able to see, to locate where everyone was seated in the van and the neighborhood. He tried to keep his attention on Eye Patch and not the moon-lit sky behind him. Ru and Wanda were in the middle seats of the large van. Tower and Colby were in the rear. In between Wanda and also sitting next to Tower, Eye Patch had his men sitting in the middle. Tower could see the door knobs on the van were gone.

"We found your GPS tracker, Mr. Tower. Nice idea, wrong person to use it on. I'm way ahead of you. Just sit back and enjoy your final journey."

"When I'm able, I'm going to smash your teeth in until they come out your ass." Tower had to be restrained by the armed man next to him.

"Just one more word and another person will pay the price."

Tower said, "Hurting women and a guy in a blindfold. That's very brave of you." Eye Patch gave a movement with his wrist as if he was done talking and the blindfold was again moved into position over Tower's eyes.

A calmness returned to Tower. "You followed them." Tower aimed his words toward where Eye Patch was sitting.

"Correct. When we were able to follow the path of the girls, and saw that they found you, I changed my plans so that you were included. You're a big part of what is about to happen."

"So you pumped up my bank account."

"Yes, Mr. Tower. Just sit back and watch how we're going to make you a star."

Bald Man stood in the middle of the living room and listened. Soft music was coming from the back of the house. He already knew the layout of the building, memorized from days of watching from his car, staring into the computer, monitoring a surveillance camera. Instead of reaching for his gun, he pulled out the eight-inch knife, sharpened each day. The handkerchief was in his pocket, ready to go. As he approached the back bedroom, the music grew louder. He passed a bathroom and did a quick inspection. A lipstick holder was on the counter, along with an array of tissues. The medicine cabinet was slightly open.

He kept going down the hallway, half expecting her to walk right into him. Bald Man was ready. He patted his pocket with the handkerchief and stepped quietly to the bedroom door.

He stopped.

The door was partly open and as he looked inside, he saw the figure in a chair by the window, just as he had seen from the surveillance camera. Just ten more steps.

The figure appeared to be asleep, her head was slumped over to one side. The sun was still ten minutes from breaking through the clouds.

Bald Man was just two feet away. He pulled the handkerchief from his pocket and held it out ready for her face.

Now.

He moved quickly, applying the cloth over her face. Something felt wrong. The soft feel of a woman's touch was not there. He searched the figure in the dim light. The head of a mannequin was staring up at him. In the chair, pillows and sheets formed a body. He picked up the head and threw it against the wall. The head rolled around as if just chopped from a guillotine. Bald Man was now a man on a desperate mission. He had to find her. He tore away the sheets, pulled all the clothing out of the closet, went from room to room throwing drawers against the wall. He went from kitchen to dining area, searching every closet.

Nothing.

He didn't know how this would go down with Eye Patch. For the next ten minutes, he thought about where he messed up. He opened the screen door and went into the back yard looking for his camera. He scooped up

the gear, then ran back into the house making one last check before he left. There was no sign of her.
He went back through the front door. During his time in the house, he was wearing gloves, so he had no concern about leaving prints. His main problem was locating her exact location.

He went back to his car and again checked the recordings from the back yard camera.

Shannon watched the bald man enter her house through the front door. The front of her clothes were still dirty from crawling on the ground, slithering like a water moccasin, hugging the ground until she reached her bushes marking the back of her yard. She kept going, still crawling through her neighbors yard, and did not stand up until she was clear of a direct line-of-sight from her back windows. She left almost everything behind. Her clothes were still on hangers. The purse, with her wallet and driver's license were still sitting on her dresser. She took the cash she had in the house and left the credit cards.

During her crawl, she took a moment to bury something in the back yard.

Her cell phone.

She put the phone in a plastic bag and dug down about ten inches. Shannon didn't have time to toss it anywhere. She left the phone behind. She also left her house, and for now, the life that was known as Shannon Tower. She would take on a new name, new personality. A new person. And all because of the one word text message. She knew were the message came from and who sent it. Shannon got a one word message to get out.

A message known only to her and Frank. Now, it was time to go. The one word was burned in her thoughts. She did not know how to reach Frank, just to get away.

She covered up the soil.

The one word: Brookstick.

Chapter 36

Tower had no idea where they were being taken. They were walked from the van to a sidewalk and eventually a hallway. He could tell by the sounds and the different types of walking surfaces. Eventually, their footsteps had a echo as if in an empty building. Each step gave off an echo, then quiet. Tower figured they were walking on a carpet.

Ten seconds later, he was pushed down and shoved up against the wall.

"Where's Tray? He needs help." Tower tried to get up and was met by two fists landing on his shoulders knocking him to the floor.

"Don't worry, we'll take care of him." The voice was not Eye Patch. Probably someone in the van.

Tower whispered, "Ru, Wanda."

"We're here." Ru answered. She sounded like she was six feet from him.

The blindfold was ripped from his face. Tower looked across the room. There was a series of television screens, perhaps seven. Each one set to a different station. Tray was not in the room.

"Where's Tray?"

No answer. Eye Patch was not in the room. The two men from the van were setting up chairs near a large table. Tower took a moment to size things up. Ru and Wands were quiet, didn't seem hysterical, just taking in the situation just like Tower. Maybe they were putting their hunting skills, as they called it, to figure out their captors. Tower could not check his watch but it had to be around 9am. They still hadn't slept, were tired, needed a bathroom and would soon smell like someone found sleeping in an alley.

"We need a piss break," Tower yelled to the two men in the room. They kept setting up wires and chairs, ignoring Tower like he wasn't there.

Tower thought about why the girls were quiet. They were witness to the violence of Eye Patch. They knew how he killed. Words and reasoning did not work. Worse, reasoning only brought on violence. In his study of the room, Tower took note there were two doors. Both closed and both had two locks. The room had a high ceiling, perhaps twenty feet. They were sitting on carpet squares, and when Tower tapped at the floor, there was a false solid feeling, like you would find in a room dedicated to computers. Underneath the floor, Tower knew there had to be hundreds of cables and wires. And there were no windows.

Eye Patch entered the room. Seconds later, Brent Solar followed carrying the briefcase. One of the men gave Eye Patch a cell phone.

"Yes." For the next two minutes, he listened. Then, "Okay. Come back here."

Solar put the briefcase on one of the long tables. He reached for a chair and sat down in front of the briefcase. Eye Patch walked over to Tower. He hunched down on his knees and leaned in close.

"I just got off the phone with my man at your house." Eye Patch was smiling. "Your wife is dead."

Chapter 37

Tower used the wall behind him to try and stand up. Before He got anywhere, Eye Patch aimed the silencer directly at his face.

"Don't even try, Mr. Tower. She's gone. Just move on. My man took good care of her."

Tower sank back down to the floor. A myriad of thoughts flashed through him. He could see someone sneaking into the house and taking Shannon by surprise. What would follow was too painful to consider.

"When I find your heart, I'm gonna rip it out." Tower snarled at him.

"You're not ripping anything. Just sit back and watch." Eye Patch turned to the women. "And don't think we've forgotten about you. I'm leaving you both to Brent. You caused him a lot of trouble. He's gonna make sure you pay for that, later."

"I'm ready." Brent Solar had a look on his face like a man about to play a concerto. Eye Patch got up and moved to the table, taking a seat near Solar.

Gripping the briefcase with both hands, Solar lifted the case so his eye was aligned with the eye reader. He stared into the square and a small light flashed green. Then he took his right thumb and placed it over the fingerprint reader. Another green light.

The briefcase snapped opened.

Solar stared into the case. He took out a small computer screen. Then two more. All three were placed on the table. Tower watched Solar lift a box out of the briefcase and set it on the table.

Once there, Solar opened the box. He took out what looked like thumb drives for a computer and stuck one of them into the collection of monitors. Tower could only see the backs of the screens. Solar never stopped smiling.

"Just a few seconds, and you'll see why you're paying all this money."

Brent Solar turned and looked at the series of television monitors behind him.

"I think we're ready, gentlemen. First let's start with something simple. Let's say a prison or two."

Chapter 38

Jervis Lanner scratched at the tattoo. The thing was new, in the shape of a fist over his upper side of his back on the left. The fist matched one on his right. He looked around at the seven by ten foot cell, the place the state put him for the past seven years. He would never get out. The mattress below him was still stained with blood from the last cellmate, the one who got cut in a fight over who would leave the cell first when the door opened. Lanner smiled and thought about the situation: a fight over getting out first. Lanner thought about it differently than most. The fight was really about who would come out of the cell last. Who would follow. The one-hundred-sixty men on the floor were all watching and they probably wanted to know who would emerge first. Who fought for that right. Lanner vowed to get it and he was prepared to die for the chance to come out of the door first. When you're imprisoned, some small things loomed large.

Lanner knew there were just hours before he would be moved to internal confinement. A place for those who broke the rules. He rubbed at the three tear drops on his face. One tear drop for each man he killed on the outside.

He stared at the small window near the ceiling. The thing was so high, he couldn't look out. Sunlight came in. And sunlight left when night replaced the sun.

He still couldn't see anything. Just the walls and the cell door.

Then, at exactly 11:19a.m. something happened that Lanner never saw before without a guard nearby.

His cell door opened.

The door clanged opened at the wrong time. This wasn't a time for moving the inmates. Carefully, Lanner looked out. All of the doors had opened at the same time. Within seconds, all one-hundred-sixty men were free to roam the three stories of the cell block. Free to look for a way out. There were no guards as usual. Nothing to stop them from getting to the second door that was only open twice a day.

From quiet to chaos.

There was loud screaming all through the building. Inmates started throwing their mattresses over the railing and onto the concrete floor below. Riot. Lanner couldn't hear his own steps as they were drowned out by the dozens of men crashing into each other, pushing down the stairs, trying not to fall and be crushed under the feet of others.

Off in the corner, he saw prison justice taking place. Two men, armed with shanks, were stabbing an inmate to death. The doomed man held up his hands, pleading for mercy, only to to be slashed and gashed. Revenge was strong on the air. Lanner joined the masses, yelling and screaming like wild dogs, free to move about, running as fast as they could toward the one door that was always locked. They got this far, maybe they could figure out a way to get it open.

When Lanner got to the bottom floor, the roar of the throng got louder. When he looked down the hallway, he knew why: the main doorway was wide open. Men were now running down the hallway. Still, there were no guards. No one to stop them.

Inside his office, Prison warden Zolen Darr was yelling so much his voice was starting to change.

"How did this happen?" He was standing at his bank of black and white TV monitors, watching inmates run from C-block in building 309.

The man next to Zolen was pounding on the bank of computer keyboards and emergency turn keys. "I don't know warden. All of a sudden the doors just opened. All of the doors. They're out!"

Zolen looked at computer monitor 27, the monitor aimed at the front gate, the doors separating the inmates from the public. Zolen's face was washed in horror. The door was wide open.

Zolen continued to scream. His right hand slammed down hard on the console. "Shit. Can't you override this? Stop them!"

Just outside the warden's office, a long hallway led to the weapons room. Six guards, all trained to be the best marksmen in the prison ran to the door of the room. "It's locked," one of them yelled.

Two guards started banging on the door, trying to find anything to smash it open. The door would not budge.

The mass of bodies running toward the outer walls was like a vast flowing river of bad intentions, ready to destroy anything in its path.

In the observation towers, two guards heard all the commotion. The panel of warning systems was blank. Communications was down. Computer screen were black.

Armed with long rifles with scopes, the towers were manned twenty-four-seven. They were ready to kill any inmate who moved into the yard without permission. Killing one person or two was was a do-able mission. Trying to stop more than a hundred men was another. They could fire and keep firing yet many would still escape.

Lanner made his way into the yard and saw four large fights, all near the small house and final checkpoint out of the prison. The doors to the house were wide open and jammed with inmates trying to get out the door.

They were fighting over who could emerge first.

Lanner made two steps and a man next to him fell dead. All direct head-shots by the marksmen. Three kicks of dirt were timed with the shots from the guards. Lanner looked up briefly to see the guards taking aim. Around him was a struggling, fighting, horde of bodies making way to the exit house. More bullets. The hard ground pinged with bullet blasts. All misses in and around Lanner's feet. Then, two more men dropped. The sirens were going now and the sound was deafening. Two guards on foot made their way into the crowd only to be set upon by two dozen inmates now armed with broken chair legs and shards of broken glass driven into the wood, with prison shirts wrapped at the ends for handles.

Lanner made his way to the front, hitting a man next to him and pulling two others out of the way. Behind him, four more prisoners hit the ground, shot dead. The bullets kept coming. He could feel the heat of the bullets zipping past his face and arms. Lanner made it inside the house, and pushed himself to the front.

Still in his office, the warden picked up the phone. "The line is dead." He pulled out his cell phone, only to find he had no bars. The cell phone was useless. "We got to stop them. What happened to the computer?"

"I don't know sir."

The warden clicked the mouse on his computer screen. "I've done everything I can think of and this piece of crap won't respond."

Jervis Lanner, convicted in the throat slashing deaths of three college students over a span of eleven months, the man with a lifetime of hard jail time ahead of him, made his way to the outside.

He was free.

Brent Solar looked like a man whose plan was coming together. Up on the monitors, Tower watched the escape. Solar had tapped into the prison's video security system and was watching everything. Only the prison staff was no longer in charge of the computer. Brent Solar was in control.

Tower had seen enough. He pushed himself against the wall, propping himself until he was standing. He ran at the table, thrusting his body like a missile toward the collection of monitors. The two men standing near Eye Patch lunged at Tower, with the trio of bodies crashing into the side of the table. Tower just missed his mark. Solar used his arms to protect the collection of tiny monitors and keyboards. Tower was subdued and carried back to the wall.

"One more move and it will be your last," Eye Patch yelled. He turned to Solar who again placed his full attention on the monitors. He watched like he was watching a video game. The grin returned. "They can't stop all of them. The police will be busy for weeks trying to round them all up." Solar turned to Tower, then back to Eye Patch. Solar had the calm of a Vegas gambler.

"An entire prison, run by computers. Just the way I like it." Solar beamed. "Everything, right down to when the toilets flush, all controlled by me." Solar looked up at the screens and the mayhem he created, rubbed his hands together and turned to Eye Patch. "Let's try something else. What about an airport."

Chapter 39

Stilton Bay International boasted almost as many flights as Miami or Fort Lauderdale. Inside Terminal B, lines of people were going through the mix of getting ready for departures. They had their carry-ons ready, their tickets and private information ready. The lines moved with the steady even pace of well-designed machine.

All of the lights in the terminal blinked for a moment. The lights went off then came back on. When the lights to the terminal flickered back to life, all of the flight information screens went blank. All incoming and outgoing flight information was missing. Each screen was blank. Passengers standing in line ready to board were stopped. A desk attendant picked up the phone and made an announcement, "I'm sorry to tell you this but we cannot fly at this time. The control tower is telling us that they cannot communicate our departure."

Kyle Wardman, senior administrator for the airport picked up his phone and spoke with a nervous tone. "Hello, this is Kyle. We have a problem. Yes, I'll hold."

He tapped the desk with his pen while staring at the clock. Sixteen minutes had passed since he first got word. "Yes. Thanks for getting out of your meeting. We have a major problem here. Somehow, we've been hacked. All flight traffic control data going in and out are jammed. All we're getting is blank screens. Yes. Yes. I'll hold."

From his office, one window looked out onto Terminal E. There, he saw passengers on cell phones, angry and yelling at his staff and air carrier desk clerks. "Yes, this is Kyle. What can you tell me on your end?" He waited for a few seconds. "What? I don't understand. How could this happen? We have firewalls, protections in place. I know. I know, but I have thousands of passengers here, stranded. I need to move these planes out of here." Kyle listened for the next six minutes then put down the phone. He got up and went to his secretary, Carol Mohannsen.

"We have to contact the media. We've got a major problem and I don't know when this will get fixed."

Mohannsen picked up a pad, ready to write. Wardman took his pen and threw it on his desk some fifteen feet away. "I'm being told the entire Eastern seaboard has been shut down. No planes in or out. Remember when a work crew accidentally cut our lines and shut us down? This is much worse. Someone has taken control of the computers. We're all getting blank screens. We can't make any connections to anything. We just can't fly like that. We're calling for a news conference here in one hour. Air travel has been shut down."

Brent Solar pushed back from his computer screens. He turned to Eye Patch. "Take a look. Nothing moves until I say so."

Eye Patch looked down. Tower could see his face lit up from the brilliance of what was on the screen. “Good. Very good. Turn up the television.”

They all turned to one of the several TV monitors in the room. A broadcaster was at the airport. The volume was turned up. “Again, airport officials are telling us that no flights are moving out of the airport. The FBI has been called in because they are telling us a hacker has successful cut off any access to flight data by anyone here at the airport. They can’t book flights, change flights, or make contact to necessary equipment. We have four reporters on this from New York, to south Florida as this is impacting every flight from the Midwest to the east coast. Nothing is moving by flight.”

Eye Patch nodded and the volume was turned down. Solar kept the business look on his face. “You satisfied? I opened the prison doors and closed down all airport travel. My little toys are working.”

Eye Patch looked at the array of thumb drives and Solar’s commuter screens.

“And they can’t trace this back to you?”

A small grin tore at the corners of Solar’s mouth. “Think of this as an internet cafe on steroids. I have developed a moving circle of IP addresses that keep bouncing all over the world. They will never find me. I can show you a few more examples if you want, but there is one thing.”

Eye Patch moved closer to him. The grin was gone. “I just upped my price. We were talking twenty million. Now that you've seen how this can work, I want one hundred million dollars."

Eye Patch did not flinch. "And what do I get for my millions?"

"Whatever you want. Just let your imagination go. It took me twenty years to develop all of this, all set up around the world. I was given access like no one else. Once there, I left back doors open for a return visit. I can do that. No one else can. And for that, it will cost you or the organization who meets the price."

"I need a bit of time to think about that. The price is much greater."

"And while you're thinking, let me do this." Solar returned to the computer screens. Tower could not see his direct movements, just his hands on the keyboards.

"Now watch. As quickly as I caused the problems, I can take them away."

Warden Zolen Darr was standing behind five of his guards, trying to make a phone call to the governor. An aide tapped him on the shoulder. "Sir, the computers are back on."

Zolan turned to the screens. Once blank, they were full of color and appeared to be back. "Lock all doors. Now!" He could hear movement through the walls. He stared at the front door. The front gate house door moved back into position and sealed shut. Seventeen men were trapped inside the small structure now unable to move.

A guard ran into the room. “Warden, the gun room is open. We’ve got weapons.”

The warden turned to them. “You go block by block, room by room and I want you to take control. If anyone and I mean anyone gets in your way, you have permission to shoot.”

“No warnings, sir?”

“One warning. If they don’t move, shoot.”

He heard the hard movement of men grabbing rifles and running down the hallway. Zolan walked to his observation window. by his count, more than one hundred prisoners were in the yard. They would have to be rounded up. Or die.

Kyle Wardman smashed his fist on the desk a second after watching the computer screen light up. Flight times and numbers rolled across like normal. He stared down. The arrival and departure boards were again lit up with information. Desk clerks were typing away at keyboards and again able to bring up information. He picked up the phone and dialed. “Yes. We’ve got control back.” He paused. “I don’t know what happened. I just know we’re back up. I’ll worry about who caused this later. For now, I just have to get going and get these flights back into the air.

Chapter 40

Frank Tower watched the display from his seat on the floor. A gun was still pointed at him since he tossed his body at the table. Ru and Wanda were still quiet, taking it all in. Eye Patch walked over to him and leaned in. "Don't even think we forgot about you."

"They'll find you." Tower said flatly as if prescribing rain coming.

"I don't think so. Our people checked him out. He has done everything he promised and more."

"They'll stop you and put you away for life."

"There's a reason I kept you up here, listening in. I wanted you to see what I'm buying. As for you, my friend, I've got a room for you."

Eye Patch motioned for two of his men to come to him. "They say you can't go for very long without water. Isn't that true?"

Tower sat silent.

Eye Patch leaned even closer. "I've got a room for you. The only water in the room will be your toilet. You can drink from that."

"What did you do with Tray?"

"He's fine."

"My wife. I don't believe she's dead."

"She's dead all right. Just as dead as your name."

A puzzled look spread across Tower's face.

"You don't understand, do you?" Eye Patch stood up. "My people do a great job of cleaning up after we, say, take someone out. They are never seen again. Everything just like before."

Tower tried to move his arms, get in a fist, only to feel the restraints. "Don't even try, Mr. Tower. Well, my cleaners left something behind."

Two men helped Tower to his feet. "You remember their friend, Stringer?"

"Yeah, the man you shot." Tower was up.

"Well, it seems his body was left behind. The police found him."

"And now they'll trace it back to you."

"I don't think so. You see, he was still barely breathing when we removed you from the building. So, we took your gun and shot him up a few more times."

The two men had to hold Tower back. Eye Patch held up his silencer and aimed at Tower's face. "We removed my bullet from his brain and shot him one more time, in the exact spot I shot him. Again, with your gun. Then we conveniently left your gun aa the scene. Nice huh?" He waved toward the door. "Be a nice former private investigator and go with these fine young men. Your gun and your bullets. Nice. I like it."

Tower was walked down a long hallway, through a set of double doors and into a warehouse, toward a box-like room made of concrete. The box had a steel door. One man opened the door and it took both of them to throw Tower inside. There was a loud clang as they slammed the door shut.

He looked around. The room was in darkness. Tower could still make out the soft gleam of a toilet seat.

No top. He could make out sources of light coming from the floorboards.

One of the men yelled through the heavy door. He was laughing. “Those holes are for the rats. You’ll hear them scratching in about four hours.”

Chapter 41

Detective Mark David drove the short distance from the morgue to Shannon Tower's house on the west side of Stilton Bay. On the seat next to him rested the autopsy report of one Maurice Stringer Benz. David stopped the car and thought about the contents of the report, the seven bullets into the body of Stringer, the shot to the head, the recovery of the gun and finally the registration of the gun to Frank Tower. He needed answers and he needed them now.

He sat outside the house for several minutes watching. Shannon's car was parked out front. Calls made to the house and to cell phones for both of them went straight to voice mail. He got out of the car and walked to the front door. After ringing three times and waiting, nothing.

Detective David walked around to the back. As he moved from front to the rear of the house, he stared into each window he passed. When he got to the back yard, he stopped. There were marks in the dirt as if someone had dragged a body. The marks ended and disappeared in the grass. He followed the path of the drag marks and inspected the rear bushes. Leaf stems were bent back. Someone was here. As he approached the bedroom windows, he stared into the large glass frame. When he reached the wall, he was careful not to touch anything with his hands. Detective David stared into the bedroom. He saw dresser drawers pulled out with clothing and other items on the floor. A mannequin head was on the floor. The bed sheets and dark brown topper were thrown up against the wall. What looked like a driver's license was on top of the dresser. No movement. He pulled out his phone and called the station for the crime techs. However, he needed a warrant.

"Something's wrong." Detective Mark David sat in the Homeland Security Office of Molissa Grant. Everyone called her Mo.

"Are you sure about this?" Grant wore a business blue jacket and matching skirt and a heavily starched white shirt. David never saw her blink.

"We've got a murder victim, a pawn shop owner with a series of past arrests for grand theft, we have Frank Tower's gun and ballistics show it was used in Stringer's death but I don't believe Frank had anything to do with this. That's not Frank."

Grant was busy writing everything in a pad. She looked up. "And Shannon?"

"She's disappeared. Along with Frank. Her car is sitting outside, her driver's license and wallet are still in the house. Our crime techs tell me they took air samples and found traces of the drug to knock someone out. I haven't heard from Frank since…"

Mo Grant tossed the pad on the table. "How long have you known Frank Tower?"

"He was my partner on the Stilton Bay force. He was a good cop until they ran him out. His mother was a slobbering-in-the-gutter crack head when Frank was a child. He saw a lot. His father rescued him and ended up raising him. He can be tough, like any cop, but he's no killer."

"You're sure about that. The autopsy report shows the blowback and stippling means the gunman was up close. That shows a certain amount of anger. What's Frank Tower angry about?"

"I just have this gut feeling Frank is in the middle of something. He came to see me before the body was found and asked me if there were any homicides yet. And then we had the bombing death of a tech company CEO and now Stringer."

"They're connected?"

"Yes, I think they are connected along with the shutdown of the airports and the prison computer freeze. I think Frank is somehow involved in all of that."

"But you have no proof of anything. Just what did you call it, gut feeling?"

"I know it's weak. But I know Frank. He contacted me once and I'm positive he will contact me again. Maybe he's in trouble."

Mo said, "I really don't think I should be contacting the F.B.I. until I know more."

She leaned forward in the chair. Behind her, David saw the sun glint off the glass on more than ten letters of commendation from various members of Congress. "Let me just say, and I don't mean to be disrespectful but why don't you let the big boys make the connections. Just stick to your little murders. You see, we deal in facts, not gut feelings."

Detective David was up and leaving the office before she finished her last sentence. What he wanted to say he kept inside. Instead, he told her, "You do what you have to do. I'm moving on with my two, as you called them, little homicide cases. Right now, it's a bunch of moving parts. I just need more time to pull it all together."

"You do that, detective. You put it all together. But just remember one thing. The airport deal was done by a pro. We can't track him to a computer IP address. And the real problem we fear is he could do it again. And in the prison escape, thirty seven inmates were shot by guards trying to run out the front. It would have been more but the other guards could not get to the rifle room. Another forty-seven inmates were later captured. And that leaves us with one. One prisoner escaped and so far, we can't find him."

Chapter 42

Jervis Lanner stood outside the shopping center, on the edge of the parking lot and away from the surveillance cameras, knowing something was building inside him, taking on shape and about to take control of his body.

The urge.

Prison had a way of putting the urge at bay. Now he was free to feed the desire. Feel the need the urge brings on. A need growing stronger with each step away from the prison, feasting on his fantasies and reveling on past murders. Seven years, he thought, was a long time. A long time away from the urges.

Removed nearly a decade, he prepared himself to go back to his hunting skills. The prison garb was long gone, replaced by a school T-shirt and jeans he stole from an overnight clothing donation bin. Still, he needed to hide his prison tats. There was nothing he could do for the tear drops. For the average person, they were tear drops. For an officer, they were an immediate warning sign as big as a billboard. Beside the need for a long-sleeved shirt, glasses were the best thing to cover the facial tattoos.

He couldn't hunt in prison. Couldn't feed the urge. Now he was free to do what he wanted.

A man wearing large sunglasses, a light jacket and plaid long-sleeved shirt, walked out of the drug store. Without staring too much, Lanner stood next to a utility pole and waited, posing as someone going over a map. Lanner was clearly in his path and he would have to walk right by Lanner on the way to the parking lot.

Lanner studied the man's hands. He tried not to stare too much to bring attention. Still, he could not stop his examination of both hands. The right hand, especially.

Perfect.

Fueled by adrenaline and power, the urge boiled up through legs and stomach, making Lanner's eyes grow big, his mouth locked up just a bit in anticipation.

He waited. Just as the man walked past him, Lanner turned and bumped into him, making sure not to let the glasses fall.

"I'm so sorry," Lanner said. "I'm a tourist. New to the area. I just need some directions."

"Sure," the man said. "Where do you want to go?"

"I'm heading south. South Florida. Any chance you're going that way? A bus station maybe?"

"Sure."

Lanner quickened his pace to match the steps of the man with the sunglasses. He sized him up. The guy was about the same height and weight. Even the shirt size looked right. Maybe next time some makeup to cover up the teardrops and he could try to use the driver's license, once he got the keys and ransacked the house for money. Lanner wanted to take him right there. Just man-grab him in the middle of the street. Give him a prison beating, then use his special talents. He held back.

Wait.

Give it time and do things right. Surely this man had a sharp knife at home. The plan was simple. Get him knocked out, put him in the car, use the license to track down the home, and find a sharp knife.

The right knife.

Then the real work on him would begin. Lanner smiled at the thought the last time he held a real knife. Not a prison shank. Get the target. Let him feel the knife.

Feed the urge.

Chapter 43

The reporter stared into the camera and on cue, spoke to a the television audience of Stilton Bay. "Police are now prepared to name a person of interest in the shooting death of Maurice Benz, known on the street as Stringer. His body was found in an apartment next to his pawn shop. Police are now saying they would like to speak to a Frank Tower, a private investigator, specializing in insurance cases. Mr. Tower has not been seen in days." The reporter turned to a man next to her. "With me, is Detective Mark David, Stilton Bay police. What can you tell me about Tower and why you want to speak to him?"

"We believe Frank Tower is key to our investigation into what happened to Stringer Benz. We have recovered a weapon and we have some trace findings that I can't share with the media right now, but this is important…" David turned away from the reporter and stared directly into the camera, "Frank, you know me. It is extremely important that you get in touch with me. C'mon in Frank. We can talk about this. There are some questions out there that only you can answer. Please, just give me a call. You know the number." Detective David stepped away from the reporter and moved toward the police department.

"And that is the very latest from the police department."

In the lobby of the Stilton Bay Storage facility, a small crowd gathered around the television resting on the counter. There were some small talk and grumblings about whether Tower was guilty.

In the back of the crowd, Shannon Tower pulled the baseball cap even lower on her head. She quickly walked past the group mixing about and pushed the door open leading to the collection of storage lockers and large air-conditioned units. Shannon did her best to avoid looking at the surveillance cameras, head down, quick steps until she reached locker 447E. She removed a key and opened the lock. The door was opened and Shannon immediately went for the small stack of cash hidden behind one of Frank's old baseball gloves. She stuffed the cash into the pocket of her jacket.

She unzipped a small black bag in the back of the locker and pulled out a new set of identification. A driver's license, four burner phones, with batteries in another bag, a bottle of hair dye, two pens and a set of car keys. Shannon gave a quick glance to see if anyone was watching her. All clear. She closed up the locker and marched, hands in pockets toward the exit door, never once looking up.

Chapter 44

Frank Tower walked the perimeter of the room, placing his hands on the wall, making a mental picture of the area, all done in the dim light. Before locking him inside the room, they cut off the cuffs. The best he could figure, the place was twenty-by-forty. A large area. The only thing he could find in the space was the toilet. Above, he saw a drop-down ceiling, so if he had a way to get up there, maybe the ceiling would provide a way out.

A single weak bulb gave light to the middle of the room. All the corners were still masked in darkness.

He walked across the room and bumped into something. "Damnit Frank, you're gonna just step on me?"

"Tray?"

"Yeah, it's me, all busted up."

Tower tried to make out a figure in the shadows and found Tray sitting in the corner of the room. He bent down to pick him up. "Don't do that. My head's not ready to be up that high yet."

"Where did they hit you?"

"Mostly on the left side of my head. I was sitting on the far right in the car. I'm still woozy."

Tower looked all around, still listening for the voice coming from the floor. "You figure a way out of here yet?"

"You saw the ceiling, right?"

"Yeah, I did. But even if I lifted you, that wouldn't get us up there. We need something to stand on."

"You okay?"

"No. Not sure what he used on me. Maybe a blackjack, but it wasn't a gun."

"You probably got a concussion."

"So, what's in the briefcase?"

Tower said, "As someone told me, d eath and trouble."

"What's he got going?"

"He pulled four small computer screens out of that briefcase, a keyboard, mouse and I think five thumb drives with enough dirty program codes to shut down airports and open prison doors."

"Wow." Tray paused. Tower could hear him breathing heavy. "How do you know all this?"

"He showed us. Eye Patch is in the room with his two men, and the girls are there."

"Did he make a move on them?"

"Not yet. They seem to be saving me for a fall guy. That's why my bank account got the pump-up job. That guy they shot, the pawn shop owner, they left my gun behind."

"Eye Patch shot him."

"They pulled the bullet out of his head, shot him up with my gun and left him for the police. I just hope Mark is seeing through all this."

"He's going to hurt those girls."

"I know."

"What about Shannon?"

"She's not dead. They would show me some proof. Put it right in my face, break me down. They said it but I don't believe it."

Tray went silent for awhile. "What is he doing with the computers?"

"You know computers better than me, but I think he's using a proxy IP address. Probably several proxies. All of them hiding the real source."

Colby sat up. "The feds find one IP location and it just leads to another. And another."

"And if he's had decades to work on back doors, the firewalls for these companies will just be a joke."

"Sounds impressive."

"Eye Patch wants to buy the whole deal. Solar has been showing what the thumb drives can do. He shut down airports from New York to Stilton Bay. Released prisoners. It's all up on the wall. On the monitors."

"If he knows his stuff, the Feds won't be able to trace him. If we've seen all this up close, our future isn't too good."

"Believe me, I know. It's just a short matter of time before they decide to cut us out of their little show. All four of us."

Tower left him and walked off the two dozen paces to the wall and reached down until he was feeling along the bottom near the floor. "We've got baseboards." Tower smiled to himself. "Just maybe." Everything in his pockets were gone, no keys or anything sharp. He took off his belt. The belt buckle had a flat surface with a shiny piece of metal and a design of a sun in the middle.

He used the edge of the buckle to dig at the top part of the floorboard. Tower kept working at it until he managed to wedge the buckle into the floorboard, and kept prying until he caused the wood to pull away from the wall. "I think I got this." He crammed his fingertips into the baseboard and with a soft crack sound, Tower separated the wood from the wall, then pulled a seven foot section away, carrying the thin, flat stick in his hand.

"I know what you're doing Frank, but what can you do with that?" Clay had a sound of defeat in his voice.

Tower carried to stick over to Tray until it touched his arm. "Man, that hurts. What is that?"

"The nails. Now, I have a weapon."

Before he had a chance to enjoy his small victory, Tower walked quickly to the door and pressed his head to the frame, then whispered to Tray. "Hear that? Someone's coming."

Chapter 45

Shannon watched the front entrance of Frank's office building for more than an hour. She sat on a bench near the main street, lined with shops and the restaurant across from Frank's now closed office window. Convinced no one was watching the place, Shannon walked to the front door and once inside took the stairs to the office.

She got out the key, went inside and immediately noticed black smudges on the desk, signs of police investigators dusting for prints. Shannon walked behind the desk, pulled out a cloth from her jeans pocket and carefully opened the drawers. A white writing pad was in the second drawer. She inspected the top page but could not make out the impressions left on the surface. She had hoped to find a name or address left by Frank. She opened the door to the back room and found a cot against the wall, full of used sheets. This had to be where Frank was sleeping these days. The apartment story was a ruse.

She smelled something. A woman's perfume. Maybe two different types, she wasn't sure. As far as she could tell, the fragrance was not in Frank's make-shift bedroom.

Shannon closed the door and left the office. She was about to hit the steps. "Hey Shannon, is that you?"

Tony Malcolm, building manager and just over four feet tall, emerged from the elevator. "Hello Tony, I was just leaving." She stopped. "You know where Frank is?"

"You, the police and everyone is looking for that guy." Tony wore two shirts, even though the temps were in the mid 80's. His stomach protruded and he had the appearance of a circus barker. "But no, he didn't leave any word with me."

Shannon studied him before asking the next question. "You still record video of people here in the hallway?"

"Yep, when it's working."

"Can I have a look?"

He nodded and she followed him to the building office. Tony worked on a tight budget. No secretary, no outgoing mail of any type yet he still maintained a certain level of security. "It's over here." He flipped open a laptop, let it boot up and tapped an icon on the screen. Four video boxes popped up.

"I've got these set, one for each day, on a twenty-four hour loop. I think this is the one you want."

He hit a spot on the keyboard and a box started showing moving video.

"Can you speed it up?"

Tony fast-forwarded. Three minutes later, he stopped. "Bingo." Shannon stared at the laptop. She watched video of Frank leaving the office with two beautiful women. They were carrying a duffle bag and a briefcase.

"The case isn't big enough for a body," Tony smiled.

Shannon glared at him and the smile disappeared. "You have video of them coming in?"

"Sure. Just a second." He moved the video back until the two woman walked into frame, headed for Frank's office door. When they turned around for a moment, both their faces were caught direct-on by the surveillance camera. Shannon studied the video. The two were in a big hurry. She watched them banging on the door and looking back as if someone was chasing them.

"Can I get stills of them."

"Sure. I can email them too."

"No. Just stills."

"Tell you what, beside the pics I can put this part on a thumb drive. If you get in front for a computer…"

Ten minutes later, Shannon was holding pictures of two women without names and the thumb-drive. "You seen them before?"

"Naw." Tony was attempting to look over her shoulder.

"The police have been here?"

Tony started packing away the laptop. "Yes, but the day they came, I was in Orlando on business."

"So, they haven't seen this video?"

"Just us."

"Good."

"You want me to keep it quiet?"

"Here's what I want you to do Tony. If the police come calling and asking, tell them about the video. Don't get yourself caught up in an obstruction charge. If police ask about me, fine, but if you don't mind, you don't have to volunteer it, okay?"

"Gotcha."

She leaned down and kissed Tony on the top of his head. Shannon left the office, armed with a few facts and still not enough answers.

Chapter 46

Bald Man walked Frank Tower down the hall toward the computer room. When they passed a large dented gray door, Tower thought he heard voices. Before he could get a fix on the sounds, the escort pushed him along, then opened the door. Eye Patch and Brent Solar were there as if waiting for him to return. They put a new set of flex cuffs on him.

"Ahh, you're back. Now we can get started." Behind Solar's back, the wall of computer screens and televisions were full of various scenes.

Tower looked around the room.

Eye Patch tracked Tower's gaze. "You looking for your friends? They're in a place where I will be dealing with them very soon."

"Don't hurt them." Tower was directed to a chair. Behind him was a white background, like a setup to take a passport photograph.

"You sure you want to do this?" Eye Patch didn't sound like he was convinced Tower should be in the room. "Just let me do this. Right now!" He raised his silencer and aimed the gun directly at Tower's face.

"I want him to be a part of this." Solar's voice was flat.

"I don't like it." Eye Patch was shouting, his voice echoing off the walls. "Damnit, he needs to go. Now."

"And I say hold off."

"Why?"

"Mr. Tower here is going to be part of my protection plan. My escape. An ex-cop. When the time comes, we'll need him."

"There's a lot of people out there to stop you," Tower said. A one-foot section of the baseboard was stuck down inside his shirt, with the nails pointed outward. He kept hoping they wouldn't protrude through the material during the walk back. Now was not the time to attack anyone. He had to size up the situation all over again.

"No one will be stopping us," Solar's tone was still businesslike. Nothing adrenaline filled. Calm. "I just want you and everyone else to see what I am about to do."

Tower sat in the chair. He had no idea where Ru and Wanda were being held. Maybe behind that door. Solar was busy at the array of computers. Eye Patch, bald man and his accomplice were standing by.

Solar looked up from his bank of computers and looked at Eye Patch. "This will be the final demonstration. Then we talk money. But before I start, I can tell you the figure has gone up."

Eye Patch's good eye narrowed with anger. He very slowly put his gun on the table. "We had a deal in place. The numbers are set. You show me this and we buy your knowledge. My customers are waiting. That's it. That's the deal. There is no more discussion."

"It's my information to sell. My years of hard work. And believe me, it works. This will be a great weapon for the biggest spender. But the bidding just went higher. I want double what we talked about."

"Absurd." Eye Patch picked up the silencer again. Barrel pointed down, he walked two steps closer to Solar. "No one changes the game. No one. Except me. The money offer stays the same. I worked this out with you and there will be no other spenders, as you called them. Just me."

Bald Man reached and tightened the grip on his gun. Eye Patch waited for an answer.

"So, you're not budging?"

Eye Patch raised the gun at Solar. "You're not in a position to negotiate. I made the terms. You agreed. The briefcase is open and all the goods are on the table. Now show us what you can do and we seal this deal."

"Okay. But I've got one thing to say. But first, let me show you this." Solar reached for a knife, then cut off the tracking monitor on his wrist.

Tower heard both doors explode off the hinges. The blasts threw him against the wall, then down to the floor. Through the smoke, Tower looked up and saw four men, all dressed in black, wearing ski masks, armed with silencers and a long rifle. Two from each door. The chest of the man next to Eye Patch lit up in bullet blasts. The four shots ripped across his rib cage leaving a tight pattern of well-aimed shots. Before he dropped to the ground, Bald Man turned around and immediately his body was hammered with rounds, making him jerk around like a rag doll, tufts of shirt and blood exploded across his chest. His gun hand not fast enough for the surprise volley of bullets. Eye Patch got off four rounds in the direction of two coming from Tower's left. All of them missed. They spent so much attention on the bald man, Eye Patch was able to get around the attackers and made it out the door.

"Get him," Solar thundered.

One man turned, steadied his hand and fired three shots toward a running Eye Patch. Tower heard the grunt of someone as if they were hit by a bullet. No sound of anyone falling. Just more steps. Eye Patch was getting away. Three of the men in ski masks ran after him. The smell of gun powder was pungent.

The remaining man in black stood in the remnants of the door, and acted as if he wanted to fire more burps toward a moving shadow. He stopped. His own men would be in the way. Tower was coughing from so much smoke. The floor was turning from brown to red. The eyes of bald man were open, locked in death.

Solar turned to Tower. "Things have changed. No one tells me what to do. No one. No one threatens me. Ever. I'm making a new deal. In a few minutes, the world will see what I can do."

He turned to the armed man. "Get the camera, we record in ten minutes."

Chapter 47

"Are you aware of what's going on?" Detective Mark David pulled the phone away just a bit in a move to stifle a shouting Molissa Grant.

"I know," he started. "Our phones are ringing off the hook."

"I want you in my office pronto. We've got to watch this thing together and get ahead of this."

Mark David said, "Any chance of stopping this, convincing the stations not to air it so we can see it first?"

"No chance. This thing will run at the top of the hour. They all got an email video. It's less than a minute. All the networks, local TV, just about every station on the east coast is airing this thing. They've already seen the video and we're told it's of national importance to put this thing on the air. If they didn't there would be consequences. They were instructed."

"Instructed? By who?"

"Brent Solar."

"So, he's using his name? Not hiding?"

"No. He's making the demands and he wants everyone to know about it."

"I'll be there in five minutes."

Molissa Grant stood in front of the large screen television. Around the conference table sat Detective

Mark David, his police chief, two local agents of the F.B.I. and several other faces David never saw before.

"There are conferences like this one all over the U.S. Our offices in New York and DC. are all monitoring this and they are reporting to the President. Since this Solar is from Stilton Bay, field agents are converging on this area from several cities." Grant looked at her watch. "We've got less than thirty seconds. Here we go." She turned up the volume of the television.

Suzzette Randell, the reporter who interviewed Detective David was on set. Grim faced, she looked into the camera.

"We bring you a special report. We are airing this in the interest of first reporting the news and second, in the hopes of saving lives. We do this reluctantly, and with the full knowledge of law enforcement. The message you are about to see was sent to us by a Brent Solar. A man who says he is the person behind the recent number of computer hacking events where a prison was opened and airport travel was interrupted. This is the message from Brent Solar."

Brent's face came on the screen. "Your channel is presenting this as a news story. This is an event happening right now and the country is involved, so please take note."

Around the table, hands were taking notes, things were being written on large yellow tablets as fast as Solar spoke. Detective David studied Solar. He was standing in front of a computer. David could not see the computer screen yet off to Solar's right, he recognized a man sitting in a chair. Frank Tower.

David got up from his set and walked closer to the screen. Tower did not speak. Did not smile. His eyes moved straight ahead and to the side.

"This message will be quick and to the point. You have already seen a taste of what I can do. Promise me, you don't want to see what I can do next. You have forty-eight hours to place fifty billion dollars into the account I will specify or I will shut down this country. Make no mistake, I can do what I say." Solar paused. "And to make sure you will know this is no false charge, look for an event to happen exactly three hours from now." He smiled, "I'm waiting."

The screen went blank. The reporter was again up on the television. "That concludes the message. We will now send you back to regular programming."

Everyone in the room started to talk at the same time. No one could make out a single conversation. They were all pointing fingers at the screen.

Molissa Grant yelled to the group. "Settle down. Okay, you see it. Ideas?"

An F.B.I. agent raised a hand. "Can we trace this?"

"We're working on it, as you would expect, but I'm told we have no way to track it down to its source. This guy knows how to bounce an email."

"What about the location?" Another asked.

"We've got our people, as we speak, going through background recognition."

A third person asked, "Who was the man sitting in the background?"

Detective Mark David spoke up before Grant had a chance to say anything. “That’s Frank Tower. By some of the briefings, I’m sure you saw his name pop up. By all accounts, it looks like he is co-operating with Solar. I don’t believe that to be the case.”

“Isn’t he the trigger-man and target of the pawn shop owner?” The question came from the back of the room.

“Yes. And there is money in his account. All very neat and it all looks bad for Frank. Still, I think he’s a hostage in all of this and he’s just playing this out until he has a moment where he can do something.” He turned to Grant. “Can you play back the message and freeze it?”

Grant picked up a remote and played the Brent Solar message, stopping at a spot one third of the way. David stood before the group and pointed to Tower’s image on the screen. “Look at his posture. In no way does he look like he’s working with Solar. Take a look at Solar’s body. He’s standing in front of Tower so you can’t see his hands and arms. That’s because he’s bound. I’m betting his hands are tied. There is no movement in the shoulders. Look at his shoulder muscles. Pinned back, stretched like he’s strapped to the seat. And look at his eye movement. He goes from the computer to the side of the room. He’s definitely trying tell us something.”

Grant stepped next to him. “Maybe he’s faking you, Mr. David. I see a man who could be a killer for Solar. We know of one dead. We still haven’t found the two women. Just maybe Solar offered him so much money he got turned.”

"I know Frank. We were together on the force. This is not him."

Mark David took his seat. Grant turned her attention to the faces around the table. "We have seventeen people arriving soon. We, along with our other offices, will be breaking into three teams. One will concentrate on the immediate threat coming in three hours. The second team will take up the issue of where to find Mr. Solar and that includes the source of where he is hacking. The third group will be on stand-by, ready to move in, anywhere he, or Mr. Tower pop up."

They started to file out of the room. Mark David waited for Grant. "You've got the wrong picture on Frank."

"Do I? And why exactly did he leave the Stilton Bay Police Force?"

"That was a misunderstanding."

"Misunderstanding!" Molissa's voice made a couple of heads turn as they left the room. "I read his files. He was accused of stealing money from the evidence room. Drug money that disappeared. It still hasn't been found."

"He was never charged with that."

"That's because he left and somehow it all got dropped."

Mark David held up a palm as if to say stop. "He was ready to strap up and take a poly. The city turned it down and let him go. Nothing was ever proved."

"And what about the mistress."

Detective David wanted to take a seat. "He wasn't-"

"Charged with anything. Yeah, I know. He was sleeping with his own client, who turned up dead. Cut up and murdered."

"We caught the person who did that."

"Did the murderer commit adultery too?"

David kept quiet.

Molissa Grant let out a sigh. "Frank Tower has bad stuff following him around. Really bad stuff. So now he's got a madman with a computer about to do-we-don't-know-what, with Frank sitting right next to him and a bank account fatter than some countries and you're telling me he has nothing to do with it?"

"That's what I'm telling you."

"Well sir, you're a bigger fool than anyone knows. You're too close to this. I'm not sure if you should be a part of this team."

"So what do you want me to do?"

"You go after Lanner."

"The escapee?"

"Someone has to handle the small stuff. We'll tackle this. You just concentrate on finding Lanner."

"I just thought…"

"You thought wrong. I read the file on Lanner. His mother used to live just outside Stilton Bay. His first two victims were found there. And we just got this." Grant picked up a file off the table and shoved it in the direction of Mark David. "And this is?"

"This is, what we think is Lanner's last victim. Twenty-eight year old male. Found propped up in a doorway. His throat was slashed and his internal organs were on the floor between his legs. That was Lanner's M.O. until police caught up to him."

"Any direction?"

"We think he's headed right here. Back to familiar territory. And one other thing. He likes to take something with him. The body was missing a right pinky finger. When police cornered him eight years ago, he had nine of them hooked on a chain he wore around his neck."

Chapter 48

"I sat here quiet, now give Tray and the others some water." Frank Tower waited for an answer. He was stalling for time and to keep three people alive. "C'mon," he yelled to Solar. "Water for us and I'll tell you what I think."

"Water. Of little value until you don't have any." Two men were still gone. Tower reasoned they were chasing down Eye Patch. Two others remained in the room. If he could just get one of them to go away.

Solar nodded to one of the masked men. "Water. But no food." The man walked through the now smashed doorway.

"Thank you," Tower said. "And while you're at it, think about letting us go."

"Go? You're not going anywhere. When they come looking to make an arrest to appease the public, I'll throw you to the feds. Yes, they know about me, but when this is over and I get away, you'll be left to deal with the charges."

Chapter 49

"I like cops. I really do. But don't take another step toward my place." Jackie Tower had a slight tremble in the finger as she pointed.

"We can talk out here. No problem." Detective Mark David took a side step and and stood out of the sun and in the shadow of a giant rosespple tree. "Have you heard from Frank?"

"You know I haven't." Her eyes were directed at the ground.

"We both know Frank is in trouble and we both know he didn't do anything."

Now her finger was pointed at David. "Then, why are they blasting him on TV. They say he murdered someone. Took money. The whole world is looking for him."

"They don't know Frank like we do."

"I know my Frankie. He wouldn't do those things." She finally stared at him, kicking the dirt with her left foot. "Sorry I can't let you in. My rehab clients have some bad memories about police. They get nervous when Frankie comes around and he's not even on the force anymore."

"I need to know what is Frank was running from? Is he by himself?"

Again, her eyes went back to the dirt. She started to step on an ant mound, then stopped.

Mark David knew the body language. She was about to lie. He could take her down to the police station, put her in a room, limit contact to the outside. He knew she had been in the station many times before as a user. Another tactic would be to just let her sit in the lobby for a hour until she decided to talk.

She tried, as best she could, to stand quietly for three seconds.

David knew Jackie was not a stranger to the waiting room of the Stilton Bay Police department. Her trail of drug use included the burglary of homes, weak attempts of pickpocketing, with success at store larceny, panhandling and multiple counts of drug possession. The rap sheet was long. There was an irony to have a son who worked on the force, in the very building where she spent so much time posing for the umpteenth mug shot. Drug users were not used to waiting quietly. This was, however, a new Jackie. A cleaned up Jackie. One who counseled others on how to step away from the demons of crack addiction and walk a new path.

He asked the question again, "Anything you tell me can help him. I need to find Frank."

He looked into her face and saw the results of time in the streets under the broil of a Florida sun. David studied her eyes and saw desperation. He counted dozens of long lines in her face and knew each wrinkled crevice had a story of guilt and deception. Both to herself and to Frank.

She was still silent.

David said, "We don't know much. Everything is under investigation. When was the last time you saw Frank?"

Jackie drew a collection in her mouth like she was about to spit, then swallowed. A wide frown carried across her face. "Those women," she said.

"Women? What did they look like?"

"Trouble."

"Where was this?"

"Here. Outside rehab. He arrived with both of them. Oh, they looked like they had just walked out of a horny man's dream. Tight jeans, high heels, make up. They were ready. And they got my Frankie into something."

"Where are they now?"

"Gone. Took off. I gave them the room in back of my place. They spent like one day there and poof, gone. Frank went looking for them."

"Were they alone? Did anyone else come with them?"

"No, but they were carrying stuff."

"Stuff?"

"Yeah, heavy bags. I don't know, I didn't pay much attention to that. I was just worried about Frank."

"Did Frank say where he was going?"

"Nope. I gave him my extra car to drive." Jackie pressed her fingers through her hair. "I don't think you're going to find him."

"Why is that?"

"Cause I think he's gone off the grid. No phone contact. No nothn', no way to see him."

"I've been looking for him. I know it looks and sounds bad but I'm not going to give up on him."

Jackie smiled. "You two always worked good together. I'm telling you all this because he considered you his friend. Please find my Frankie."

"I'll try. Can I see the rooms?"

"Sure. Let me get the key."

Once he got the key, Detective David snapped on a pair of gloves and very slowly moved about the room, looking for anything. In one room, he found hair strands. Black ones. He picked up one and noticed the strand felt fake, like one from a hair piece. He didn't want to disturb the others. Let the crime techs take their photographs and collect what they need. He stepped back and out of the small house, then approached Jackie.

"Listen, if it's okay, I'd like to have the crime techs check the rooms, look for DNA, anything to help us find him."

"Okay." Jackie looked as though she was trying to remember every last detail. "You are right about one thing."

"What's that?"

"Seems like they were running away from someone. Someone bad."

"The two women?"

"Yes. I got the feeling Frank was hiding them, keeping them safe."

"Okay. Thank you."

Jackie turned to leave. "Have you stopped by his office?"

"Yes, but we didn't find anything."

"You talk to the building manager?"

"He wasn't there when we-"

"You might want to talk to him. That man knows everything about Frank."

She stepped out of the shade of the tree and into the grill of the midday sun.

Chapter 50

Detective David was driving when the cell phone rang. "David…"

"Detective, this is the warden where Mr. Lanner broke out. You have a minute?"

"I'm driving but go ahead."

"Sir, we're not positive on where he is going but all indications are you folks down there should be ready for him."

"We've been briefed. What can you tell me about him other than what I read?"

"Well sir, he was a quiet inmate for us, most of the time. I say most, because certain things would set him off. Our phycologists here think he was manic depressive and a sociopath. No regard for human life."

"What caused that, if you know." David was three blocks from Tower's office building.

"He's been in institutions since he was twelve years old. His father once beat him up so bad he was in the hospital for three months. Spent three weeks in a coma." The warden could be heard picking up a stack of papers. "Says here, he got beat because he was sitting in the doorway and blocked his father from getting to his mother. Wanted to do his daily beatdown. Kid blocked the way, kid got beat."

"Nice."

"He carries that possession thing even now. He beat up a prisoner for getting in the cell doorway. The one thing we still can't figure out is why he has such a fascination on hands and fingers."

"I read that. He takes a finger from all of his victims." David was about to park his car.

"Yep. Pinky. During trial, psych evals, questioning, everything. We never got out of him what was the deal. All I know is please be careful, he's about to reach his old territory and that's not good."

"Thanks warden. I appreciate it."

Chapter 51

Only one gunman was watching Tower. Solar was stepping over bodies and collecting his computer and putting monitors into the briefcase. Tower ran the facts over and over in his head. The three others in black were still out looking for Eye Patch. If he could just somehow get his hands free, he could use the nails and board inside his shirt. Tower had a reasonable idea of where the women were being kept. Now it was just a matter of waiting for the precise moment. Still that moment would have to come soon before the others came back.

"We've got to move soon." Brent Solar was talking over his shoulder. Tower noticed something. He was placing wires in and around the room.

"Where are we going?" Tower asked.

"Always the man with the questions. You'll find out soon enough."

"What are you doing?"

"Don't worry yourself with my intentions. Just sit tight and everything will be fine."

"Are you placing your bombs?"

Solar turned around. "A few bits of wires and you know everything. Yes, this place will become a pile of ashes."

"What about Tray and the women? They should be going with us. You'll need them as hostages."

"No, Mr. Tower. I need you. Your man Tray and especially the women can be part of the rubble. I only need you. Not them."

Solar ran wires around the room leading out the door. He left for a moment. The men in the ski mask raised his weapon, pointing the business end of the silencer right at Tower's forehead. A drop of perspiration rolled down Tower's right temple, stopping at his cheek.

Solar returned. "At first, I thought, leave the place booby-trapped for the police. Believe me, eventually they will figure where this place is located. Then I thought, why not surprise everyone."

"So, this is your surprise in three hours?" Tower tried again to free his hands. Nothing.

"No. This is just part of the sideshow. The surprise is something else." He moved closer to Tower. A bright smile seared across his face. "Time to see the Pearls. I want to play with them a bit before we go."

Tower tried to thrust himself at Solar. "Forget it. You're not going anywhere." Solar moved away and left the room.

Moments later he heard a door open and close. Listening to the number of steps taken by Solar, Tower knew where the women were being kept. Right where he figured, just outside the room where Tower was located.

Brent Solar went straight to Ru and grabbed her face with his right hand. Both Ru and Wanda were sitting on the floor, their arms forced into an upward position as their hands were tied and hoisted unto a hook.

"Someone special from out of town. Isn't that what you said?" Solar was yelling at Ru. He stood over her, his hand stuffed into his pocket as if he had a weapon. "Someone special. I am someone special! Special enough to make you suffer some of what I had to go through when you took my briefcase."

"We didn't know anything about that case." Wanda tried to take his attention from Ru.

Solar moved in front of Wanda. "I remember what you said. That you'd been watching me all night. I bet you were. Setting me up, taking my money, drugging me so I couldn't fight back."

"Sweetheart, it was just business. We don't mean to hurt anybody." Ru was twisting and moving her wrists, trying to free herself. Tired, she gave up.

"They almost killed me because of you two. I had to beg for my life. And now I want you to beg for your life. Go on, why should I keep you alive?" Solar slammed his hand against the wall above Ru's head. "Your bar man got his melon blown up. Head clean taken off. Is that what you both want? A bullet to the back of the head?" He pulled out a small vial. A few pills rattled around in the plastic container. Solar shook the pills in front of Ru. "You gave the drugs, didn't you?" He kicked her leg. Ru gave out a low moan.

"Leave her alone." Wanda shook her arms but could not break loose of the hook on the wall.

"I tell you what. I stuff some of these pills in her and then I finally get to see what's in those jeans."

"I'm not swallowing anything." Ru tried to move one leg on top of the other as though tending to the kicked area. "You can't make me take anything."

"Oh no?" Solar pulled a .22 from his waist. He slowly removed the suppressor. "I want you to hear this bullet. I don't want to hide it. You take those pills or what's-her-name, Wanda, gets a special delivery between the eyes." Solar moved closer until the barrel of the gun was just touching Wanda's forehead.

"Leave her alone," Ru said. "I'll take them."

"No," Wanda was shouting. "Don't do what he says. Leave her alone."

Solar smiled the smile of a man who made the final chess move. "That's it. You take these pills." He put down the gun, removed the cap and spilled two pills into the palm of his hand, then moved closer to Ru. "I've been waiting a long time to get reacquainted with you. Your friend can watch."

Solar used his left hand to force open Ru's mouth. She tried to move about, shaking her head, anything to stop him.

Tower heard the muffled cry of someone being jostled and trying to fight back somewhere down the hallway. Sounded like Ru, with her polite southern accent. Now was not the time for politeness. Tower turned all of his attention to the gunman standing six to eight feet from him.

Tower rocked his chair back and forth until he fell on his left side. The nailed piece of wood scratched him just above his stomach. When the gunman walked over, got close, Tower kicked with both feet, knocking the gun away from him. The man left Tower to retrieve the weapon. Tower wrestled out of the seat and kneeled a bit until he could step through his arms until his tied-hands were now in front of him. Tower ran full speed into the other man. He pulled the nail board from under his shirt and drive the wood into the man's neck. The masked man reached for his neck. The gun was still a few feet from them. The ski masked man swung twice at Tower, missing both times. Tower was swinging the board, making the other man concentrate on another hit rather than reach for the gun. Tower angled himself around until he was between the gun on the floor and the thumb-drives on the table. The masked man would now see his dilemma. Protect the computer or go for the gun.

The man chose the gun.

Tower cut him off, smashing his hands into the man's face, driving him backward toward the table. The board dropped to the floor. Like a football player driving back a defenseman, Tower pushed him back and into the table with the valuable contents of computer equipment and the briefcase. The thumb-drives rolled off the table. One of the computer monitors also fell. The sound of the cracked screen echoed off the walls.

The hurried sounds of Solar's footsteps were heard down the hallway. Solar entered the room and ran for the computer parts on the table and floor.

"Get him," he shouted.

Tower fell to the floor. Now both the masked man and Tower were wrestling over the gun. Neither could get a good grip on the weapon. Tower was slowed by the plastic cuffs on his wrists. Solar was too busy with gathering his computer to enter the fight. Tower managed to get his hands free and again smashed his fists into cheekbone. The move gave him just enough time to grab the silencer. Tower aimed the gun, while trying to stand up. The man in the ski mask backed off, taking steps backward until he bumped into Solar.

A smile started at the edges of Solar's mouth. He aimed his 22. Tower fired a shot, missing both men and tore into the wall. The aim was a bit off with the cuffs on. Tower's trigger finger moved quickly. Another burp. The second round hit the masked man to the right of the heart. He dropped to the floor near the body of the bald man. Solar grabbed the weapon, snapped the briefcase closed and ran for the door, firing as he charged toward the doorway. He used the briefcase as a shield.

Tower ducked behind the table and fired off four more burps. The silencer gave no kick. The first two bullets chipped wood and tore holes into the wall, all just missing Solar. He was gone. He stopped and turned around. A red light on small box was blinking. Tower did not know how much time he had but he had to get Tray and the others out before the blast.

He gave up on Solar and went inside the room just a few feet away. Inside, he found Ru and Wanda, both sitting with their hands tied, their arms kept in an upward position with the knot snugly resting on a hook. They looked drained of energy.

Tower eased the knots off the hook, freeing the women. "Let's go. We don't have time. There's a bomb."

The three of them ran to the room where Tray was being kept. Tower opened the door, ran inside and helped Tray to his feet.

The four made their way to the sight of daylight far on the other side of the building. They were blindfolded when they arrived, and Tower had no clear idea of a good escape route.

Behind him, he could see the masked man coming at them. He was slowed by the bullet wound. Tower sized up the area in front of him. "I know where we are," Tower studied the expanse of concrete and bare walls. "This is the Conjunction Building."

Tray studied the room. "You're right. Slated for demolition. The place has been empty for months."

Tower kicked up his pace and ran toward what used to be the lobby. Work crews were long gone, the floor was a pattern of ripped tiles and cut marks from crews tearing up the place. They got to the front door. Tray ran ahead of him and was about to step outside.

"Stop!" Tower shouted.

"We can't. He's right behind us."

"Don't step on that." Tower pointed to a large metal plate on the ground. A single wire ran from the plate and continued up the wall, almost out of sight.

"It's a trap." Tower looked around. He directed the three to a window near the entryway. Tray first, then Ru and Wanda, all four climbed through what used to be a large window overlooking a patio.

"Keep running," Tower told them.

They got forty yards away when the ping of a bullet hitting the ground made them stop.

"Cover," Tray yelled. Ru hid behind a tree. Wanda found a broken sign warning people to stay out of the area. Tower looked back to find the masked man standing in the doorway, taking aim.

"He found another gun," Tower said. "But he can't step on that plate." Tower put his hands to his mouth and shouted. "Get back. It's a bomb. Don't step outside."

Tower's warning was met by four more shots. The bullets hit all around him. He took cover next to Tray.

"It's no use. He's not going to stop." Tray started to pull on Tower's arms.

"I'm not giving up." Tower rose up out of stooped position and waved his cuffed hands in the air. "Don't move. There's a-"

The blast knocked him to the ground. Tray held on to a large metal pipe as the ground shook from the explosion. The air rained down with bits of concrete and hot pieces of plastic. Smoke rolled over them like a ground cloud. Off to his right, Tower heard Wanda coughing. Ru came over to them. Her clothes were dusted in debris.

Tower checked the door. The masked man was gone, all part of the rubble of a two story building.

"We've got to wait for the police," Tray told Tower.

"You wait. I've got work to do."

"Stay. We can all testify you didn't kill Stringer."

"That clears me for one. I've got more explaining to do and now is just not the time."

"How can I get in touch."

"Don't look for me. Just tell them everything that happened."

Tower leaned down and picked up a piece of glass, handing the shard to Tray. "Cut me loose."

"Not staying?"

"Cut me loose."

"There's one problem." Colby directed Tower to turn around.

"We're not staying here." Ru was holding the gun Tower retrieved from the man in the ski mask.

"And what are you doing?" Tower asked.

"My daddy took me hunting on his trips. Taught me how to shoot. We're going with you."

"Stay for the police."

Ru kept the silencer pointed at Tower. "And explain how we ripped off someone and took a duffle of money? I don't think so. Where you go, we go."

"I don't know how this is going to turn out." Tower looked over his shoulder for police cars.

"We can always take off when we see a chance, but for now, we're traveling partners. Your friend can stay and tell police what he knows, which I'm guessing does not include anything we did."

"No." Colby dropped the glass on the ground. Tower shook free his hands.

"You're sure about this?" Tower could hear the faint sound of a siren approaching.

Wanda said, "All I know is, we're leaving with you. So, let's move."

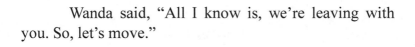

Chapter 52

Tower reached for the weapon. “Before we go, give Tray the gun.”

Reluctantly, Ru handed the silencer to Colby. “What we don’t know,” Tower started, “is how many homicides are connected to that gun. Better let the law figure it out.” He turned to Colby. “I’ll be in touch. Not sure when, but I’ll be in touch.”

“No problem.”

Tower sized up Ru and Wanda. Their shoes were scuffed up. Ru had a rip on her jeans on the left hip, exposing skin. Her hair was a jagged collection of blonde strands pulled together by her hands. The blouse was torn in two places. Wanda had a small cut in her right arm. For both, makeup was a long ago memory, with no lipstick, or eyeliner. They were covered in a layer of dust. Tower flashed to a moment when they were standing on a roadway in heels and tight-fitted dresses.

“You ready?” He asked them.

“Yeah, let’s go sweetheart.”

They left Colby standing at the edge of a destroyed building, wafts of debris dust still curling off from what was left of the front door. Fire trucks and two police cars passed them. They kept their heads down and continued walking.

Less than a half-mile from the scene, Ru stopped, turned her back to the traffic and held out a thumb.

“What are you doing?” Tower insisted.

"Getting us a ride."

A minute later, a van stopped. A door opened. "C'mon," she said. "Let's go."

The driver was pushing eighty years old, tapped a faded Marlins baseball cap when Ru smiled at him and Tower was barely in his seat when the man dropped his right foot on the gas pedal.

"Thanks for the ride, sweetheart," Ru let the charm spew from her eyes. Tower kept an eye on the road. A phalanx of police cars, bomb squad truck and fire rescue units rumbled past them going in the opposite direction.

"Somethin' big happened, that's for sure." The man directed all of his comments at Ru.

"This is a nice van you have." Ru ran her fingers down the arm rest, until she touched the man's right hand. "I bet you have a nice big house."

"Used to, don't anymore. Sold it."

Tower grimaced. The man was spending too much time staring at Ru and not on the road ahead. Twenty minutes later, the sounds of sirens and police cars were long gone. Tower tapped Ru on the shoulder, nodding it was time to get out.

"Here?" Ru's voice had the sound of protest.

"Here." Tower turned to the man. "Thanks for the ride. We appreciate it."

The man pulled over. Ru got out, staring at her surroundings. Wanda adjusted her wig. Both of them waved to the van driver.

"Okay, why drop us off in the middle of nothing." Wanda turned around, as if trying to figure a direction to take.

"We're walking one block, then a left and we're there."

Both turned to Tower. Ru walked to keep up with him. "The place is called Brookstick."

Chapter 53

Mo Grant watched the fire crews directing hoses, as streams of water arced into the sky hitting hot spots where flames still stretched several feet into the air.

Detective Mark David walked up behind her.

"They're not here, if that's what you're about ask." Grant took out a small pad and started writing. "Tower's tech guy is being debriefed. From what he says we got more than one body under that pile and we've less than an hour until Brent Solar makes his next move."

"Anything about Tower? What's his name, Tray Colby?"

"Nothing. From what he says he was locked up most of the time with a bash on the head. The man we want Tower, decided to take off rather than help law enforcement." She took her time with the last few words.

"If Tower's not here, I'm sure he had a good reason."

"Not wanting to go to jail does that to people. I will tell you this…" She pointed to a command truck thirty yards away. "If what Colby is telling us is true, Tower is cleared of the pawn shop owner. Says this guy with an Eye Patch did the shoot. Not Tower."

"I believe him."

"And you haven't even talked to him yet. That sure is loyal."

"I just know that kind of move is not Tower's way of doing things." David stared at the van.

"I don't like this." Grant put her hands on her hips. "Solar could be anywhere, about to do anything."

David handed Grant a picture. "What is this?" She examined the photograph.

"Take a good look. It's Tower and the women."

"Where did you get this?"

"From the surveillance video taken in the hallway outside Tower's office. You can see a duffle bag and a nice expensive briefcase."

"Any word on where they were going?" Grant did not take her eyes off the picture.

"No. The building manager wasn't there at the time. But you can see they were in a hurry. That jives with what Tower's mother told me, that he was sheltering two, very attractive women."

"So, what's the connection to Solar?"

"Not sure yet, but somewhere these women bumped into Solar and the result was not good. They've been running ever since. I believe Tower is in the good guy in all this."

Grant continued to study the photograph. "What do you have on the women?"

"Well, the one, Ru Stanner, had a restraining order on a bad husband until one day he came calling, armed with a gun. She outmuscled him for the weapon and winged him."

"He's alive?" Mo studied some paperwork.

"Far as we know. Haven't tracked him down yet."

"She face charges for that?"

"No, self-defense."

"And the other one?"

Detective David took a moment, as if mentally going through his notes. “She never had it good anytime in her life. The only thing we have on her is some field cards from officers visiting her house. Her mother had a lot of men over. Noise complaints. She also had a bad boyfriend. Pounded on her till she finally took off.”

“And what about now?”

David pulled an envelope from his jacket. “Take a look. They were picked up three times and questioned for thefts. At no time did any of the victims want to press any charges. They all changed their minds and said nothing was taken.”

“What do you think?”

“I think the men were too embarrassed to say what really happened. How do you explain that to a wife?”

Grant held up the envelope and video evidence.“ Can I keep all this?”

“It’s all yours. I’ve got more. I emailed your office a copy of the video.”

“Thanks.”

David looked at the ruin in front of him. Dark fire clouds circled off and trailed toward a bank of clouds. “We’re sure Tower’s not in that mess?”

“No. He got away. But we’ll catch him.” She smacked the notebook against her side. “We’ve got people on notice from New York to Miami but we’re still not sure if we can stop Solar.”

“Did we get anything on him from the airport computer attack?”

"Not enough. We have the anti-terrorism computer unit on this. It's like he has a daisy-chain of IP addresses we have to weave through. We're going in circles and we can't find the source. We think we've closed up the firewall issues but we're not sure."

A fireball erupted off to the right of them. Fire crews aimed their water arcs in the direction of the newest hot spot. Grant looked at Detective David. "The clock is ticking but we're just not ready. We don't have enough intell to know where he will strike."

Chapter 54

Tower surveyed the place. Bright yellow letters stretched across the front of the building. Cream of the Cream. Two couples were planted in seats set up outside. Tower directed Ru and Wanda to a table far from the front door.

"I thought you said this place was called Brookstick?" Wanda picked up the menu, then put it down. "We don't have any money."

"This used to be called Brookstick. Named after the owner. When he died, the daughter sold the place. New owner changed the name. I still call it Brookstick."

Ru looked around. The pace was slow. Somewhere behind them, they could hear the buzz of an unidentified bug. "We need to be moving. Why are we here?"

"Just be patient." Tower leaned back in the chair. A waiter, a woman in her early twenties, rested two glasses on the table. Her dark hair was pulled back. The hair matched her eyes. "I have to bring one more glass. Can I get you something?"

"Give us a minute. The water will be fine," Tower nodded a thank you.

"Okay. I'll be right back."

Before she left, Wanda downed the entire glass of water. The waitress noticed. "I'll bring a pitcher."

Tower checked his watch and tapped the table. "You two okay?"

Ru rubbed her arms like she was removing slime. “Him touching me? I kept thinking he was going to kill us.” She took a sip of water. “He was trying to drug me, and telling us he wanted her to watch. I was about to make him squirm until you walked in. Thank you very much.”

“He kept saying he wanted to finish what we started.” Wanda kept looking up the street as if Solar was about to appear.

The waitress returned with the pitcher of water. “Y’all ready to order?”

“I hate to be a pest, but we need just a few more minutes.” Tower pushed the water toward Wanda.

“No problem. I’ll be back in a few.” She walked off, her hair bouncing against her back.

He looked at Ru. “So, you know how to shoot?”

“Since I was nine. Shotguns mostly. There isn’t much call for a gun in our line-of-work.”

“How did you two get started? You know, in your line-of-work.”

They both looked at each other as if waiting to see who would speak first.

“Support group,” Ru volunteered. “The group taught us to be independent. Work on our own, for ourselves.”

“We were both in a battered situation.” Wanda kept rotating the glass of water in front of her. “We don’t hate men, don’t get me wrong. But it just seemed like they kept taking from us.”

Ru placed her hands on the table. “We were sitting in a bar one day and it just hit us. We can do this.

We can take what we want. The next day we sat in the same seats, dressed to kill and things happened."

They both broke out in a laughter Tower had never seen before. Wanda rolled her eyes. "We decided to do some taking. It was too easy. Seduction and conquer. Until we got that briefcase."

"Any idea what was inside?" Tower questioned.

"No way sweetheart. We just wanted the money and the watches. Period. We thought there was papers in there. Documents. We had no idea."

Tower leaned back again in the chair. A haze settled over the street and the palm trees growing out of the sand-filled dirt. He figured the dust cloud from the explosion had moved across the city and clouded the air. Sun glaze on the surface of the road gave false impressions of water on the gravel. Out of the filth-laden air, Tower saw something. The movement of the hips caught his attention first. The sway of hips and legs brought him directly to an image of a person he first spotted on a beach in the Bahamas. Now Tower was locked onto the woman moving closer. He was staring now, hooked on the angular face, the way each of her steps hit the ground, soft and purposeful, with the ease of a dancer. She emerged out of the hot street and kept coming toward Tower until he could see the sheen in her eyes. When she stopped, she pulled the cap from her head and let her hair shake down in a cascade around her neck. Then she leaned down and kissed Frank Tower with the passion of three hundred hearts. Shannon Tower breathed a deep sigh and looked at the faces sitting at the table.

"I'm sorry to say this but all of you really need a shower."

Chapter 55

Lanner tapped on the map. He smiled. There was a circle around Stilton Bay. He tossed the map into the car and leaned against the fender to start his favorite pastime. People watching.

All kinds of people walked by him. Tall, short with fast steps, pudgy stomachs, all colors. Lanner didn't seem to care. He just wanted to study their hands. He reached into his pockets. Fifty-seven dollars and ninety cents. The money was stuffed back into his jeans and he heard the rattle of the car keys. Lanner turned around and focused on a group of people watching a television inside a diner. There was so much attention on the TV and he walked across the street to hear more.

Inside, the man behind the counter was turning up the volume. The reporter was making more of an announcement rather than delivering news lines.

"We just got the second message from a man who has identified himself as Brent Solar." The reporter was working from a stack of notes. A picture of Solar was over her left shoulder. "Solar sent an email instead of a video. In it he says the incident will take place in approximately five minutes. And that he is waiting to see if the government will deliver on his earlier demand of thirty billion dollars. That was the end of the message. Everything we have received has been turned over to federal authorities."

The report over, the place was full of

conversations. People giving opinions on what to do, leave or stay to eat. Half the place emptied into the street. When Lanner heard two people say they were headed to the gas station, he did the same, driving his car to a station a block away. He was the first one in line at the pump. Behind him, the line stretched around the block. Panicked drivers got out of their cars and waited.

Lanner gave the clerk inside fifty dollars. Half-way through, the pump stopped working. Lanner looked around him. All the pumps had stopped. He looked inside to find the lights were out. Lanner walked a few steps until he could see down the block. All traffic lights were out. Car drivers were honking horns. Stores were without power. People streamed out into the street. People were yelling. Angry drivers left. One man with a gas can threw the container against the wall.

Chaos was about to ensue.

Lanner smiled.

Shannon gave Tower a gym bag. "I brought you something. I've got some burner phones in there. Some cash, keys to a car which is parked on the other side of the road, a passport if you need it and your backup piece."

Tower reached into the gym bag Shannon brought with her. He grabbed the Glock and stuffed the gun under a towel. "Thanks."

He turned to Wanda and Ru. "Ladies, I want you meet my wife, Shannon."

"They said you were dead," Ru said.

"Not dead. By the way, we're separated."

"Hope it's not our fault." Wanda stared at the both of them.

"Naw. Happened long before you two came along. Although you did say these were your clients…"

"Just that. Clients." Tower stepped around until he was in Shannon's face. "I didn't think you remembered Brookstick."

"We had a long talk, remember. If anything happened, if you needed to really warn me, gather up that bag and go back to the spot where we had our first real date. The name changed but the place is the same."

"What are you going to do?" Tower slung the gym bag over his shoulder.

"Now that I know you are okay, I'm going to Detective David. I haven't done anything."

"You're helping a fugitive. Me." Tower injected.

"Far as I know, you're not charged with anything either. Beside, legally I'm still your wife. They can't get anything out of me."

Tower looked at the women at the table. "You trust me with them?"

"No. Even though you smell like a pig's jockstrap, I think either one of them would jump your bones."

"One already tried. I'm not interested. They're my clients. That's it."

"You've done it before."

Tower took in a chest full of Florida air. "I was trapped into that situation." Staring down, he noticed he was talking with his hands to make a point. Tower stacked his arms across his chest.

"Yeah, I know, she went after you until she wore you down. But the point is, you finally gave in. I can't go through that again. Not now. Not ever."

"That," Tower said, "will never happen again. I promise."

She studied his face. "Been waiting for you. I've been staking out this place since I left the house."

"Did they hurt you?"

"They had a man watching my bedroom. I caught on, then I found your message. That was enough. He tried to get to me but I was out the back door. Some bald guy."

"He's dead."

"You?"

"No. Solar has his own hit team. The bald man got in the way. Now Solar is running things by himself. Putting the country on notice and if he doesn't get his way."

"I know. bad things."

Tower leaned in to kiss her again. Shannon backed off, then joined him in the kiss. She was the first to break away. "Frank, be careful."

"I'm going to look out for my clients. Till the end. That's it."

"We'll see."

The waitress approached them. "We have a problem. Electricity is down all over. We can't do any meals right now, I'm sorry."

Tower said, "I think it's beginning."

Chapter 56

Tower saw the image of Shannon growing smaller in the rear view mirror. He checked the gas tank. Full. Ru sat in the front seat with him. Wanda stared at the scenes unfolding around them. None of the traffic lights were working. Stops at each intersection became a nightmare. Drivers out of their cars, yelling at other drivers. They saw four accidents. Fire trucks were stuck in the long line of cars. People didn't want to let others through.

"Where are we going?" Ru asked.

"We have to get a change of clothing." Tower passed a bag back to Wanda. "Eat something."

The waitress had given them a bag full of pastries, half a cake, loaf of bread, a pound of deli meats and a six pack of soda. "We must have looked desperate," Wanda said.

Tower drove around two cars, almost hitting the second. "That, plus a fifty dollar bill will get you something."

Block after block, buildings were dark. Lobbies were full of people, faces pressed to the glass doors, as if deciding whether to enter the street or stay in their offices. A few places still had light. Tower reasoned they were on backup generator power.

Tower moved down a side street and found little traffic. "We're going to the flea market. It's just outside of Stilton Bay. Most of the venders use cash. No cash register. I think I can talk my way into a shower somewhere. We get new clothes and then where're off.

"To where?" Wanda asked.

"Solar does everything for a reason. Everything. There is a reason why he picked that abandoned building. I'm going to find out why. And when I do, I'll know where to find him."

Tower clicked on the radio. A reporter was in mid-sentence talking about the power outage. "That's because authorities have no idea how the entire power grids on the East Coast are all down, from New York to Key West. All because of the hacker-attack by the man identified as Brent Solar. If you can hear my voice, police departments have called in all off-duty personell. All fire fighters have been called back into their respective stations. Some cities have volunteers at intersections. At other locations, drivers have gotten out of their cars to direct traffic. The governors in seven states have called for the National Guard. We are trying to confirm reports that the President will speak to the nation in thirty minutes. Although, we don't know how much of an audience there will be since most don't have power."

Tower turned off the radio. "Won't be long before the thugs start throwing bricks and walking out with anything they can get."

Two blocks later, a man with a hand gun was sitting in front of his business. A sign rested against the wall with the words: NOT MY STORE.

"I can wait on the shower. What's your idea." Ru was staring at the scenes unfolding as they headed into downtown Stilton Bay.

"We're here." Tower parked the car. He pulled the Glock from the gym bag and handed the gun to Ru. "I'm going inside. I'll be at the clerks's office where they record building permits and documents."

"What on earth are you doing there?"

"Playing a hunch. Don't let anyone take the car. I'll be right back."

Chapter 57

There was one man behind the counter on the third floor of the Stilton Bay Records Department. Tower walked the stairs since the elevators were not working. People were leaving the building like crowds leaving a baseball game.

"We're thinking about closing. Is there anything we can do for you? As you can imagine, our computers are down." The man appeared anxious but calm. He wore a food stained gray plaid vest over a white shirt and no tie.

"You have family to check on?" Tower looked over his shoulder at the empty desks.

"No. My one son is on a cruise. Probably doesn't know anything about all this. What can you possibly need?"

"Two things," Tower started. "For one, I want to look at the permitting for the demolition on the building…I forget the name."

"You mean, the one that blew up?"

"Yes. That one. Are the records handy?"

"Fortunately, we keep a lot of paper files. Let me see what I can find." He disappeared to the back of the large room behind rows of metal cabinets with large drawers. Out in the corridor Tower heard footsteps and worried voices, all headed for the stairways.

The man came back with a set of drawings, and a one-inch thick file. "All yours. If you see anything, I'm afraid we don't have a working copier right now."

"That's okay. I'll just take notes. Thank you."

Tower opened the plans. The demolition company was very thorough with a detailed seventy-day plan to first empty the building, tear it down, rather than use explosives and debris removal. Tower took note of a signature on a company stationery. He pushed the plans away and concentrated on several letters from the company to the city, laying out certain facts, including the company no longer needed the building and decided the fourteen acres were more valuable and salable without the structure. And that several buyers would then be interested.

"Thanks, sir. The company that owned the building moved into a new place six years ago. A five story building. Do you have those plans?"

The man thought for a moment and put a finger on his lip. "Oh, I don't know if I can do that."

"Why not?"

"Well, that company went through all kinds of discussions with the city to seal those plans as much as possible. "

"Are they here?"

"Well, yes."

Tower pointed to the window off to their right. "Do you know what's going on out there? People are scared. Someone is attacking us through computer tactics and we're not sure how all this is going to end up but what you have in that drawer over there could be extremely important. I'm a private investigator. My name is Frank Tower. I used to be a cop in this city. What I find, I will tell the authorities. Now, if you would be so kind, please direct me to the right place." Tower didn't mean to raise his voice.

"I'll tell you what, I'm not telling you directly where they are, but if someone were to look at row J, drawer number seventeen, that person might just find something like what you were describing. I'll stay here and not get involved."

"Thank you." Tower opened a small door and went around the counter, looking for row J. He found drawer number seventeen and pulled it open. There was one large file, with a seal over the flap. Tower broke the seal, opened the package and spread out several pages on the top of the three foot high cabinet. He took out his smart phone and captured a picture of the section he was seeking. Tower took three more pictures, then put the documents back into the file. He closed up the drawer.

On his way out the door, Tower thanked the man behind the counter three times.

Out in the street, three cars were blocking the intersection. Two drivers were arguing. When Tower got closer he saw two cars were involved in a major accident. He got inside his car.

"You find what you were looking for?" Wanda turned her attention from the accident to Tower.

"Just maybe, but I think I know where to find Brent Solar."

Chapter 58

Molissa Grant put the phone down with the softness of lowering the lid of a casket. She turned to Detective Mark David. "I was just informed this is about to get worse."

Grant got up from her desk, lit up now by four battery driven lights. "I pulled you away from the escapee situation because you know Tower. He is one of the best contacts we could have to finding Solar."

"You say this could get worse. What do you mean?"

Grant pushed a lock of hair back into place."Maybe I'm wrong. They're calling me back in a few minutes. We released Tray Colby. Have you spoken to him?"

"Yes. As you said, he cleared Tower in the Stringer homicide and right now, other than an explanation on the money in his account, we have nothing to get him on."

Grant's face braced with lines. "Yes, but we still need to talk to him. Now."

"I hear the power is coming back on in places?"

Grant looked up at her ceiling and the darkened ceiling tiles. "We're still out but yes, power is slowly going back on in most cities." She paused. "We have a problem."

Grant got up from her chair and went to the board in her office. With no windows in the room, she was cloaked in shadow. Always accustomed to speaking in front of her board, Grant's words came out of the dim light. "You see the file on my desk?"

David looked down at the thin file.

"Go ahead," she said. "You can open it."

He reached for the file and one single piece of paper slipped out of the cover. David started reading.

"That, detective, is the latest and final warning from Mr. Solar."

"But this says…"

"I know what it says. And the deadline passed ten minutes ago."

"I thought he gave us more time than that."

Grant stepped back to her desk and into the reach of the temporary lights. "He changed up everything. Took a day off the demands and is about to unleash the next part of this."

"This, meaning a shutdown?"

"This country is not going to be held up by terrorists, no matter where they come from, here or abroad. We held firm on his demands and the money was not exchanged. We are not paying him."

"So where does that leave us?" David put the paper back on the desk.

"That leaves us with one hand down in the foxhole and we don't know what we'll find when we bring our fingers out."

"So, this one bank is being targeted."

Grant took the file and placed it in her desk. "He's hacked into the computer system at the bank. Right now, the computers are being slammed with commands, so many commands from different IP locations that the computers can't handle it, so everything is shutting down." She put her hand on the telephone. "Even with the power on, the tellers can't do transactions, no one can make a deposit or withdrawal, and wire transfers are impossible. The call I am about to take will confirm that what is happening at this one bank will be spread to many other banks across this country. That is, unless we get Solar his money."

David let his anger show in his voice, "That's the best our negotiating team can do?"

"Correct."

Chapter 59

Tray Colby grimaced. The young doctor stopped working on him. "You okay?"

"I am now, thanks to you." Above them, the light flickered again. Only certain lights in the hallway were lit. The doctor again put his hands on Colby's forehead and shined a light into his eyes. "You sir, had a small concussion. A bit of rest and you should be okay." The doctor tapped one of the IV bags hanging on a holder. "Some more fluids and you should be good-to-go in about two days."

"I don't have two days doc. I have to get out of here in a couple of hours."

"We got our generator working. You're much better off here than out there." The doctor looked out the windows at the street where the traffic lights were out and cars zoomed through the intersection just missing each other like small-town race cars on a Saturday night.

"I can't explain it but I have to go."

"That's against doctor's orders." The doctor stayed at the window as if transfixed by the scenes in the street.

Colby sat up straighter in bed. "You see what's going on out there. It's a mess. One guy is holding the country hostage. I've got to get back out there."

"Then let me get you some pills to take with you."

Molissa Grant stood in the debris field of the downed building and turned to Detective Mark David. "Cadaver dogs got three hits. We pulled three bodies from this pile of crap but not much else." She turned to the still smoldering chunks of metal and concrete. "Anything here to give us an idea of where he is now?"

"No." Detective David looked at the crush of debris as if it would talk to him. "Where do we stand?"

"The banks are still closed. The President and FAA stopped all air travel across the country. The National Guard was called out and we've got several check points at various places. We're not worried about soft targets. Solar doesn't seem interested in killing masses of people, he just wants our attention."

"And our money." The detective looked at the pile. "My gut tells me he's still very close by. That he's in a secure place somewhere just ready to watch the chaos he's caused. But where?"

Grant packed a few papers into a briefcase. "I'm headed to a command center they've set up at city hall. You coming?"

"Yes. I'll be there." He reached into his pocket and pulled out his cell phone. The stare was long. "Wait a minute!" Detective David stepped over the rocky ground and pushed his phone in Grant's direction.

"This has to be from Tower."

Grant took the phone. "Does it mention his name?"

"No. Just says he's checking something out. Will let me know if it is legit."

"You believe him? Could be a diversion."

"No. It's a burner phone. Doubt if we can trace it, but it's him."

Chapter 60

Tower drove past the building twice and parked the car a block away. "I've been past here a hundred times and never really noticed this place."

He looked out on the front walk-up. A security guard shack was empty. Two small signs warned the public to stay out, private property. There was no company sign. No logo. And like much of Stilton Bay, the place looked abandoned. People were in the street, driving out of the city with no real direction as far as Tower could tell. They were just driving. One person went on TV and said the West Coast was not hit yet. The proclamation sent thousands packing the expressways and turnpike with no real promise gas stations would be open.

On the way Tower passed two gun shops. The doors had been ripped open and the places looted. If Solar wanted calamity in the streets, he got it. Tower got out of the car and leaned against the warmth of the hood and front fender. "If I told you two to stay in the car-"

"We're going with you." Ru was getting out of the front seat as she spoke.

Wanda, sans wig, ran a hand over the soft Afro. "We're in this."

"Okay." Tower pulled the Glock from his waist. "If I wave you back to the car, then you go. Is that clear?"

They both nodded.

Tower stepped toward the building. "Let's go."

They were twenty feet from the car when the first bullet tore into the pavement, inches from their feet. Tower looked up. "Run. Now!" They ran for cover, using a smashed taxi cab as a shield. All three hid behind the yellow car with shattered windows. "I didn't hear any shots," Wanda yelled. She was kneeling down and looking upward at the arrangement of three tall buildings across the street.

"The snipers could be anywhere up there," Tower studied the buildings. One was a condo and looked empty. The other two were office buildings. All of them six stories tall. A good man with a scope, silencer and rifle could take them out anytime he wanted.

There was a slight hissing sound and the right front tire of Tower's car flattened in an instant with the impact of the bullet. They watched as strike after strike, bullets lit up the side of the car, shattering windows, blasting the other exposed tire, blowing the handle off the door, smashing the side-mirror and tattooing the entire side with quiet blasts. The car sank down on one side, tires on rims.

"Could be three of them up there," Tower kept checking the top floors for any sign of muzzle flash or glint off the gunman's clothing.

They were pinned down. Tower turned to them. "They're showing us their firepower."

Ru kept her head down."Well, it's a lot. We're trapped."

Tower checked the layout. As best he could determine, the blasts were coming from the center building of the three. He checked and saw three windows appearing to be open. The gunmen would have the rifles set up on tables and off from the window itself.

Tower took aim at the center windows. The Glock, efficient and worthy, could be heard echoing off the building. The first shot ricocheted off the wall, missing the window by two feet or more. The second shot must have hit the mark.

"I got them thinking." Tower prepared for a response. "Now, they're pissed. Get ready and stay down."

A flurry of bullet blasts tore into the exposed side of the taxi cab. More than one gunman was shooting at them. They couldn't hear the muzzle blast, only the results. Bullet after bullet crashed into the cab, others bore into the dirt around them. All missing them. For now.

Wanda yelled. "We can't stay here."

They were one block from the entrance to the nondescript building. Tower looked down the street. An assortment of utility poles, a row of palm trees and one ficus tree gave the only hint of cover.

From Tower's right, he heard a familiar sound. The sound grew louder. He looked down the street. The wide front of a Stilton Bay transit bus was heading in their direction.

"Perfect," Tower said.

The bus kept coming into view. The driver did not have on a uniform and there did not appear to be any passengers in the front of the bus.

"Okay, here's what we do." Tower gave Ru and Wanda instructions. The bus continued on its path.

"Where is he going?" Wanda glanced up quickly then went back into her position, leaning hard up against the cab door.

"Not a bad idea," Tower said. "You could live in that bus. Put provisions in there. Store fuel. And be mobile."

There were no shots fired. Tower figured the snipers probably heard the same thing, a bus coming into the fire zone.

As the bus moved in front of them, Tower, Ru and Wanda moved from their position behind the cab and run up along side the bus. The driver, wide-eyed and white-haired, kept waving his arms from Tower to get out of the street. They kept coming.

Tower did not have to wait long for the snipers to react. The first bullet hit somewhere in front of the bus. The driver stopped.

Bad idea, thought Tower. More bullets rained on the street. Quiet makers of death, each bullet claimed a spot. Bus windows, a mirror, a rear quarter panel. Bullets pinged against metal.

The driver acted as if he didn't know what to do. Tower directed Ru and Wanda to board. In order to do that, they had to put themselves in the line-of-fire. Tower raised his Glock and started firing. "Now!"

They ran under the protection of Tower's volley of gunshots. The driver opened the front side door of the bus and started to drive off. Tower was still outside, firing away.

In unison, Ru and Wanda yelled for the driver to wait for Tower. "I can't wait. I got you. That's enough."

Outside the bus, Tower grabbed a mirror still intact and held on. The bus driver kept going. Bullets pinged against the side of the bus. Tower kept firing in the direction of the snipers. Another eighty feet and maybe they would be out of direct range.

Tower felt his grip slipping on the mirror. His feet were dragging on the street. The tips of his shoes were being worn down, like leather on sandpaper.

A bullet hit just inches from his face. The bus moved faster.

Tower saw a figure run out of the building and take aim.

Eye Patch.

He held the rifle steady. The shot missed. The doors opened and Wanda pulled Tower into the bowel of the bus. "Thank you," he said.

"No problem, Sweetheart."

Once settled on his feet, Tower turned to the driver. The man looked to be mid-thirties, an inch under six-feet tall, wearing jeans and a torn black T-shirt. "I thank you for the ride."

"To be honest, I didn't want to stop."

Tower turned to his left. The back of the bus was filled with boxes. "Where are you going?"

"Mister, my entire business is in the back. I took this bus but in the chaos, no one seemed to mind."

"Again, where are you headed?" Tower watched as the man never moved his eyes off the road.

"Home. Trying to reach my wife. Get the heck out of here."

"You can still do that, but we need your bus to make one stop for us."

Chapter 61

Rolando Persperia walked so fast, his assistant could not keep up with him. “Who discovered this?” Persperia yelled to the man three steps in back of him.

“The main bank president noticed it first. Checked on the balance of the Murcko and well, you’ll have to see for yourself.”

Persperia wiped across his brow, yet the beads of sweat kept coming, rolling down his cheek and leaving the back of his neck with a sheen of moisture. “How could this happen?” He noticed he was talking to himself. The man behind him was now twenty feet back with the distance growing. “C’mon, you fool, the whole country is depending on the Murcko. You know what this will mean?”

The assistant was in a full run and caught up to Persperia as he was about to enter the main office of the bank president. He opened the door so hard, the ten-foot tall hand sculptured work of art slammed against the wall, rattling in the jamb.

“What is going on here?” Persperia was again in speed mode, walking around the large desk, angling himself in front of a computer screen.

Alahandro Cruz, the president of the bank thrust his arms in the air. “We are ruined. Ruined, I tell you. It’s gone!”

Persperia tapped the computer keys hard, giving off a loud clacking noise. “What do you mean, gone.

There's four billion dollars tied up in the Murcko. It is the main way our people pay their bills. They trust the Murcko. What happened?"

Cruz pointed to the computer. "We've been hacked. Overnight. Our analysts tell me someone used a back door and transferred all of the money in our accounts."

"To where?" Persperia shouted.

"We don't know." Cruz looked at the marble floors. "We have no choice. We have to tell the people."

"There has to be a way to get it back. What do our people say?" Persperia was still hitting keys as if money would suddenly appear in the coffers of the country. "Twelve million people have used the Murcko for decades. We never had a problem like this before. Never! I have to tell our public something. What about our friends, the Americans? Maybe they can help us."

"They have their own problems." Cruz took out a cigarette. He had promised his wife the smoking would stop. Fifteen months without so much as a puff. Now this. Cruz tapped at the cigarette like it was an old friend. "We will both be run out of office. The country will be bankrupt. We will have to borrow money from a kind-thinking country. If we can find one. There is no way to explain this away." Cruz took a drag on the cigarette and coughed so hard, a spittle of blood settled on the tip of his tongue. "Who cares about what the cigarette will do," he said. "When the people get word of this, they will think we stole the money. And then they will come after us."

Persperia picked up the computer and tossed the thing to the floor, smashing the monitor, parts snapped off and rolled under the desk. "I am going to find who did this."

Cruz sat down, letting his body fill up the void in a favorite chair. "The Americans say the man is up front about being a computer thief. His name is Brent Solar."

Chapter 62

"Where do we stand?" Detective Mark David stood by the door as if he was about to leave at any moment.

Molissa Grant took a deep sigh. "Well, the deadline passed and we are getting our ass kicked."

Detective David looked at a board full of papers and metal clips to keep them on the wall. The area was lit up by four battery powered lights. Grant continued her assessment.

"He hit the national bank of one country, taking a few billion from what they call the Murcko. It's a form of a credit card system that allows people to pay bills, get cash. He wiped it out overnight."

"Man," David whispered to himself.

"He did the same thing in three other countries. That's not all." She threw a stack of papers on her desk. The papers were in the midst of dim light. "That, sir, is the list of exchanges where some of the most sensitive wire transfers are telling us seventeen-hundred money wires have been compromised." Grant took another deep breath. "At last check, they were missing almost two billion dollars." Her fist came down hard on the darkened desk. "If he keeps this up, he'll easily surpass the amount he asked for. And if the banks and exchanges that are not hit, well, they might as well close down. Just who would trust them. We're all going to go back to the age of keeping our money stuffed in mattresses."

“What about the anti-hacking and computer virus units?”

“Nothing yet. Solar has been moving very fast. He gets in, leaves no trace of having been there, and what’s worse, unless we stop him, he can re-enter anytime he wants.”

“What’s our role?” David was opening the door as he spoke.

“This is all in DC’s hands. We’re just one of the little guys now. Fourteen banks have been broken into in the past four hours. They break in, yet they can’t do anything. The numbers and locks have been changed through the computer. Solar did that too. We’re at his mercy. There’s a conference call I have to take in about fifteen minutes after the President gets briefed. The airports haven’t seen Solar. The road checks have turned up nothing. He hasn’t sent a message. We are all waiting. However, all forces of this country are all over Stilton Bay looking for him.” She paused and looked at the wall of paperwork. “We are in a lot of trouble and I think we’re very close to giving him what he wants.”

Chapter 63

"I think our best chance is to enter through a second story window. Bypass the front doors. If he's in this building, he probably has cameras watching." Frank Tower stood in the shadow of a fifty-foot tall oak tree. He turned to the bus driver. "I know this is going to sound off the wall but I need you to drive right past that building, up on the sidewalk and give me a few seconds to get through a window."

"Sure, I can do that."

"What about us, Sweetheart?"

"You can stay here." Tower checked his Glock.

Wanda looked at them. "We're going with you."

"I don't think that's a good idea."

"Hope you don't mind," Ru said, "But it's not an option. Eye Patch is just a few minutes behind us. We're not going to wait here."

"Okay. But you have to do exactly what I tell you, is that clear?"

"Clear."

Tower pulled the driver aside. "I'm hoping they're going to be so busy, they won't pay any attention to you. Once you drop us off, you can go. And we thank you a great deal for what you've done already."

"No problem. Does this have to do with the man causing all this?"

"Yes. But it's out of your hands once you drop us off. Okay."

Tower turned to Ru and Wanda. “How did Eye Patch know where to find us?”

Both of them looked down at the ground. No answer. Tower stared at Ru. “There was a time when I wasn’t in the room. You talked with him, didn’t you?”

Ru didn’t speak at first. Then, “We were threatened. They threatened to kill you and your friend. We had to do something.”

“Did he promise you money?” Tower glared.

Wanda spoke up. “We didn’t have much choice. The offer was money and our lives. And yours, if we co-operated.”

“That co-operation ends now. Or as of now, you’re not my clients anymore. Which is it?”

“Sweetheart-“

“No sweetheart. Drop it. What did he give you? Some kind of tracking device? A phone? What!”

Ru pulled a cell phone attached to what looked like a GPS. “He gave us this.”

Tower took the device. “So, he knows we’re here?”

“We turned it off,” Ru said.

“Doesn’t matter. He can still track us.” Tower took the small GPS and placed it on the ground. With a hard step, he crushed the tracker under his shoe. He took out the guts of the device and tossed them into the holes of a sewer grate. “You want to leave now? We can call it quits. You’re on your own.”

Wanda looked into his hard stare. “We don’t want you to go. We thought we were helping. We were wrong.”

Ru stepped toward him. "We're survivors, Mr. Tower." She turned around, lifted her dirt-stained blouse and exposed her back, showing Tower two long scars. "That's a present from my ex. A little strap lashing for absolutely nothing." She pulled the top back down. "What we both do is survive. Yes, we agreed to take the tracker. Yes." Her shouting made Tower wince. "We like men. We really do. But we both decided to take advantage of their indulges."

Wanda pointed to Tower. "You know what are indulges? It's that moment away from the wife when you see a pretty face and one drink leads to two and then you're in a situation with another person and all thought about the wife goes away. Indulges. You have any indulges, Mr. Tower?"

Now it was Tower's turn to stare at the ground and not answer.

"We fulfilled those desires you have in the corner of the room," Wanda continued. "When you think no one is watching, when your carnal desires take over."

Ru smiled at Tower. "What about your carnal desires?"

Tower said, "I never said I judged you."

"The men we stole from were all stealing moments from a wife, a girlfriend." Ru's voice was filled with exhaustion. "That's why they never complained to the police. They were caught. We were doing their wives a favor. Trust me, they never strayed again. Not after we drugged them down and took everything they had." She pulled again on her blouse and tucked the edges down into her jeans. "So, we have no regrets about the thing from Eye Patch. We worked out a deal with him. And he never thought Brent would turn on him like that, killing his crew."

"Get one thing straight," Tower started. "Both of them are out there to kill us." He turned as if ready to make a move, then stopped. "I'm not better than the men you ripped off. I'm guilty of what you called my indulges. I admit that and I'm still working through it."

Wanda and Ru turned with him. Wanda grabbed his arm. "That's why we're going with you. Put an end to this. That's what survivors do."

Chapter 64

"Who found the car?" Detective Mark David stood on the top floor of the Stilton Airport garage, overlooking a tram parked six stories below. A blue car, with a dent running down the side was angled in the corner of the lot. Molissa Grant watched as two crime techs dusted the door knob.

"We got a call from a parking attendant, just as he was about to go home. Says two men got out of the car. One looked just like the guy on TV, he said. Brent Solar. He lost sight of him."

David was just feet from the row of police officers on the roof. Another team of twenty officers was in the main terminal, along with the dogs, going through bathrooms, gift shops and all sections of the airport, including luggage racks and the belt carriage. The airport was at a standstill. No traffic, in or out. Passengers were told to stay away because of the hacked computer system and the loss of general power. A backup generator was in place, yet security would be compromised. A decision was made to close the airport down.

"He could have made his way to one of the sixteen passenger jets and commandeered the thing," Grant spoke to Mark David, however her gaze was fixed on the crime techs and the car.

"Anyone check the trunk," David said.

"First thing. Nothing of value in there." Grant turned to him. There was a rare moment of desperation in her eyes. "This lead better turn into something. Our time ran out and we have no answers."

A man in a blue suit walked up to Grant and whispered something to her. He stepped back and walked toward the stairs. Grant pointed to the car. "The attendant isn't one-hundred percent positive on the ID. We did a photo line-up."

A crime tech started yelling for Grant. She walked a quick pace to the back of the car. Mark David followed. "Look at this." The tech was holding a thumb drive. "Found it stuffed in the back of the trunk."

"Nice work," she told him. Grant snapped on a pair of gloves. "We got something to plug this into?" The tech produced a laptop and helped her plug in the drive. Within seconds, he opened the icon. They listened to a message.

"If you've found this, then please know I've left the country. I'm in a remote spot where the air is cleaner than a newborn's breath." Grant stopped the recording. "Well, is that him?"

Mark David nodded. "It's him. We've got to check flights as best we can. He must have taken off in all the confusion. We check our people in the tower?"

"Yes," Grant said. "They don't remember any flights at that time, in or out. Somehow though, he left." She continued the recording.

"If you're trying to figure out where I am, leave your energies to other pursuits, like staying alive. You went past my deadline. Now you'll all have to pay. And that still does not remove my demand. Put thirty billion into my prescribed account and I'll stop. That also means you stay away. And since you disobeyed me, you can get ready for a new round of trouble. I will restore the power at exactly 2pm. That will show you I have some good qualities. People will be able to get gas, go to the bank, keep their food cold. Everything will be as normal. But soon after that, everything will change again. I promise you. Unless I get my money. Oh, and one last request. Please let the media play this message."

"What happens now?" Mark David asked.

"We play the message to the world and we keep looking for him."

"No payoff?"

"I doubt it. We have to find him."

Chapter 65

Frank Tower looked at his watch. 1:55pm. “We go inside in fifteen minutes.” Exactly 2pm, the traffic lights came back on. Tower, Ru and Wanda snapped around to see lights in buildings, the whir of air-conditioners start off in the distance. “We got power back,” Tower exclaimed.

Their host, the driver of the bus took out a small portable TV. “Just let me check,” he said. He turned on the tiny television and all of them crowded around the device. They heard a reporter come on and introduce the audio clip with Brent Solar’s voice. “Yeah, that’s him,” Wanda yelled.

Ru waved her hand as if to quiet Wanda. They listened to the message, heard Solar’s voice saying power would be restored. Once the audio was finished, the reporter finished with a sentence saying the government would not be giving in to Solar’s demands. No money would be sent his way. And sometime later that evening, the President would address the nation.

The reporter then started to report on a long list of places giving out free food and on the many shelters opening and offering people a place to stay.

Tower looked at the three. “There’s something wrong.”

Wanda stared at the television. “For once, I agree with you. Why would he restore power?”

“He’s up to something,” Ru hand stroked her hair.

Tower said, "The reporter said sources say he's out of the country."

Ru looked down the street at the monolith of a building. "So why are we here? That place looks deserted. There's no cars in the lot. The lights are back on everywhere, but that place still looks dark. Are you sure about this? I think we're in the wrong spot."

Tower studied the building. "Solar is misdirecting everyone. He wants people to feel secure about going back to normal. But why?"

The driver of the bus coughed before he spoke. "Maybe he means what he says, that he's showing some compassion."

"He doesn't have any compassion." Tower stepped out of the bus. "He's planning something. We missed the deadline and he's about to make his next move. We've got get inside that building."

"Sweetheart, you sure about this?"

Tower readjusted the positioning of his Glock in the back of his pants. "We're going inside."

Chapter 66

The bus driver steered the bus into the parking lot, as if he was lost and about to turn around and leave. He made a U-turn in the lot and on the way back, drove close to the building. Once the bus stopped, Tower, Ru and Wanda made their way up through the roof hatch of the bus and crawled out. Tower took out a small knife and went to a window closest to him. He dug around the edges until the window was loose.

Without saying anything, he worked as quiet as possible, working into the edges of the window, scraping away the elastic liners until he felt the corner was weak enough. Using bathroom plungers found in a vacant store nearby, Wanda and Ru pushed the suction cups onto the glass. Together they carefully removed the glass pane and set it on top of the bus. Tower first, all three entered the office building. They took up positions inside the office and remained quiet.

The bus pulled away.

They heard the rumble of the bus fade in the distance. Tower pulled out his Glock. He would be the point. Ru had a position on the right, Wanda on the left. Tower scanned the room. There were no lights on in the place. He walked to an air vent. No AC. The office was the standard with up to twelve cubicles so everyone in the area could see other employees simply by standing up.

Tower pointed to the door leading to the hallway and elevators. He walked a quick yet quiet pace to the door and stopped. Tower listened for any movement. Nothing.

Seven minutes passed and Tower sat there in the dim of the room, light only in spaces lit up by sun beams and waited. A thunderbolt of a thought him. He turned to Ru and Wanda, the whispered. “What if your money has been tied up in the banks for days and you weren’t able to get at your cash.”

“I’d be more than eager to get it out,” Ru said.

Wanda leaned and looked around the corner of a desk. “And the first chance I got to pull some money out, I’d do it.”

“Exactly,” Tower started. “Most of the country has been denied access to their money, so now that the power has been stored and the banks computers have been freed up-“

“There will be a run on the banks,” Run completed the sentence.

“So what?” Wanda leaned back against a wall.

Tower said, “The so what is that if millions run to the bank to pull money and Solar is just waiting to redirect all those transactions, we could have a disaster.”

“He can do that?” Ru questioned.

“If he was able to redirect money wire transfers, I think he can do just about anything.” Tower got up from his position on the floor. “We have to move.”

Tower opened the office door. Quiet. If his reading of the building plans were correct, Solar would be on the first floor in a room with no windows. Glock pointed in the direction of the hallway, Tower moved a few steps, all the time keeping his back to the wall, eyes forward. Ru and Wanda trailed him by five yards. He reached an exit door leading to a stairway. Tower opened the door slightly and waited. No one there. A quick scan of the stairwell offered no sounds. He waited a full three minutes before moving. Tower started his way down the stair, Glock in the shooting position, eyes moving, roving over the rail. No men in black masks.

He reached the half-landing and stopped. Still no movement. Tower nodded to Ru and Wanda for their descent down the stairs. Once all three were with Tower, he slow-stepped down to the first floor.

He stopped at the door.

Tower pressed his right ear to the door and listened. A .22 silencer could be on the other side. Carefully he cracked the door a half-inch and let the warm air rush against his face. The possible outline of a male shadow hinted someone down the hallway about twenty feet. The plans for this section of the building were locked in his memory. Three doors, a bathroom and the room where he suspected Solar was hiding. Glock first, Tower eased out of the stairwell, taking up a position along the wall. He had instructed Ru and Wanda to wait for a few minutes. If they did not hear a scuffle, they were to follow.

Tower made the walk to the first door. Nothing. He kept going. The door in question was just around a corner and to the right. The only door down the corridor. Tower got as close to the corner as possible without making the turn. He checked the hallway. Without question, there was a solitary shadow just around the turn. Tower retreated. There was a quick conversation with Wanda. Tower checked a door next to him. A turn proved the door was open. He went inside. Ru and Wanda moved back down the hallway, and found a bathroom door. Watches synchronized, all there waited another four minutes. Exactly.

Wanda removed a metal tissue holder from the vanity and from a distance of about three inches, she dropped the holder.

She quickly moved back inside the bathroom.

The major part of the plan meant Tower would have to open his door precisely when the guard walked by. Tower waited. He didn't have many options. A gunshot in the hallway would be deafening and result in Solar bolstering the door. A surprise entry after that would be impossible. Tower would have to take him by hand. The steps outside the door were soft yet not without some sound.

Tower waited. Then opened the door.

The man in the black fatigues and mask had just passed him to answer the Wanda-made noise in the bathroom.

Perfect.

Tower got his hands around his neck, choking him down and held him until he was no longer moving. He dragged him into the room behind him and searched his clothing. Tower moved the silencer off to the left. A check of his pockets, and inside his body armor turned up nothing. He unwrapped the mask.

Tower was certain he saw the face somewhere before but could not place him. He removed the mask, pants and bullet resistant vest and changed clothes. Tower would take up the spot by the door.

He entered the bathroom and Wanda almost attacked him until she realized Tower's half-smile.

"I'm going to put this mask on and move to the door. After a few minutes, I'll go inside. Here, take this." Tower handed Ru his Glock. Tower took the silencer. "If I need any help, I'll call for you."

Ru smiled the smile of a bar moll about to make another score. "I've got a different angle. You want to hear it?"

Chapter 67

Clad in the black fatigues and mask, Tower held the silencer up to the back of Ru's head. Without knocking, Tower turned the knob and entered the room.

He stepped inside, pushing Ru in front of him.

Brent Solar turned around. "What do we have?"

Tower had a decision to make. There was no way he could mimic the voice of the man now put down and silent in the room down the hall. He also didn't know any code signals set up by Solar and his men. Would he say something or just stay quiet? Tower chose to say nothing.

"Found her outside? Very nice." Solar moved away from his work. Before him was a wall of monitors, much like the setup in the vacant building. Solar was wearing a gray suit, heavily starched white shirt and a bright red tie. Yards behind him, a TV camera was set up and blank wall was lit up by a row of lights, all implying where he would be taping his next address for demands.

He walked up to Ru and smiled. "Got away from me before but that won't happen again. How did you find me? And better yet, where is Tower?"

Solar turned to the masked Tower. "You find anyone with her?"

Tower shook his head. Then he raised the .22 and pressed the end of the silencer directly against Ru's temple.

"How does it feel," Solar asked.

Ru stared directly at Solar and smiled back. “Feels like I got you cornered.” A look of puzzlement traced Solar’s face. Tower pointed the weapon at Solar.

“Again, how did you find me?”

“What’s important is that you stop what you’re doing.” Tower took one small step forward, all the time trying to amass the number of Solar’s armed men. “Right now!”

“Maybe we can work something out.” Solar glanced quickly to his right. From behind a row of equipment, three men emerged, all with silencers, one with an AR-15 rifle.

“Here’s the deal,” Tower said. “The first bullet is reserved for Solar. The rest can take your chances with me but your boss won’t be around to see the finish.”

“Some deal,” Solar responded. “I’ve got a better one. What about you put your gun down and I won’t steal-“

“Bank money,” Tower cut him off. “Bank money from millions of people. And all wire transfers. I know what you have planned.”

“We have a real stand-off.” Solar rested his hands on the table. Behind him, the three men spread out, making it more difficult for Tower to watch all of them at the same time.

“I checked the workups at the planning office.” Tower took a step to his right. “I saw the plans for this room with your name and initials. They actually let you in charge of the reconstruction on the floor?”

“They told me they were giving me an important job. No one else wanted to do it. A shit job for someone who got passed over year after year." Solar turned to the vast arrangement of monitors and computers. "I made this my own. No one came in here. I remodeled the floor but I kept this room for myself."

"I knew you would come back here." Tower never took his eyes off Solar. "You needed a place for your servers."

"Ah, you figured it out."

Behind Solar, more than a dozen floor to ceiling computer servers flashed lights. "The brains," Solar said. "My baby. No one goes near them. No one."

Tower pushed Ru behind him. "Think for a minute. These people you're about to steal from, they didn't do anything to you. Your boss did that to you. You killed him. You got even. Now shut this down. Don't go forward with this."

"You're about to see history, Mr. Tower. When I start this in motion, billions will transfer just like that." Solar snapped his fingers. "They won't know what hit them."

"Just like you hit my bank account?" Tower kept the weapon directly at the middle of Solar's forehead. A bullet there might stop any brain function and hopefully any physical move to transmit a command to the computers.

"I thought you'd still be spending that money. But yes, thanks to my departed friend with the Eye Patch, yes, I pumped a lot of money into your account. I was new at this and I wanted to see if I could make it happen. You should be happy."

"Just stop what you're doing and we can all walk out of here."

"That's not going to happen." Solar slowly moved his finger toward the keyboard.

Tower got ready to fire. "This is your last warning. Stop right now."

From behind Tower, out in the hallway, he heard scuffling, like two people gripped in armed combat and smashing against a wall. Solar must have heard the noise. His eyes darted briefly away from Tower's gun.

The next few moments would be a blur.

The grunt of a woman's voice struggling with someone was undoubtedly Wanda. Ru left Tower's side and retreated back toward the door.

A single shot from the AR-15 tore a fist-sized hole in the wall just above the door. Tower theorized the man who was put down and presumed out cold in the other room was awake and in the hallway. In a quick moment Tower knew he was wrong.

In the hallway, Eye Patch was at Tower's back, fighting off a spirited Wanda with Ru joining the scrum of flying arms in all directions. One thing was clear. Eye Patch was able to track them down and he was armed. Tower turned to see the hallway. Solar moved in close to the keyboard and the computers.

Tower got off a shot, just missing Solar's shoulder and catching the ski-masked man on his left, directly in the left arm.

Two targets. One decision. Tower could move back into the hallway and engage Eye Patch or he could stay on Solar and move in. Ru and Wanda were making

Eye Patch use all of his energy to deal with the two of them so Tower again refocused on Solar. When Tower turned again in his direction, Solar must have ducked down because he was no longer in a direct line-of-sight.

Tower fired at the ski-masked man on the right while running toward Solar's last standing position. The silenced bullets made a muscled poof sound. The man on the right moved behind a server for cover. Tower looked up to see Solar running between the tall servers, holding a wireless keyboard. Tower fired off two more shots. One banged off a server, causing a chuck of computer parts to fly off into the air. The other bullet moved past Solar, just over his shoulder.

Tower ran after him.

The man on the left, bleeding from the bullet, aimed his weapon at Tower. The move ended quickly as Tower let off a shot, hitting the man in the head, just above the eye. He went down.

Tower glanced back. Ru was thrust up against the wall. Ru was starting to slide down the right side of Eye Patch. In a few seconds, he could dispatch both of them. Wanda found her gun on the floor and tried to aim the Glock up at Eye Patch. The man with one eye knocked the gun away from her. He shoved both of them off and ran in the same path Tower had taken.

Solar made a fast quick turn when he came to the end of the servers. Tower stayed in pursuit.

Just one more look behind him. Tower saw Eye Patch move over one corridor of computer servers as if to get ahead of Solar. Then came the loud noises. While Wanda held a gun to ward off anyone, Ru started smashing every computer, every monitor she could find. Finally she just used the Glock, firing at each piece of equipment in her vision.

Tower turned the corner. No Solar. He moved slow and steady at the back end of the large room, checking each row. He had to be here. In the background, Ru could be still be heard on her mission.

Tower found Solar.

He was desperately trying to hit a series of key strokes while running. Not easy. Tower fired off another silenced round. This time, the bullet nicked the corner of the keyboard. When Solar ducked left and away from Tower, he found himself standing face-to-face with Eye Patch. The one-eyed demon raised his weapon toward Tower.

"Your ass is about to get shot." Eye Patch smiled.

From somewhere off to his left, a shadow was closing in on him. A shadow with blonde hair and a determined look.

"This is for Stan and Stringer." Ru let the Glock rock. The side of his shoulder took the first hit, turning Eye Patch in Ru's direction and now exposed to a full onslaught of incoming fire power. His chest popped with small explosions, each tiny hit produced an irregular wound of blood and tissue. Ru kept firing. She was still pulling the trigger over and over as Tower reached in and grabbed her hands. "You're out of bullets," he told her.

Even after Tower removed the Glock from her hands, Ru was still firing an imaginary gun, her face was lined with taut muscles, her eyes flared, the chin rigid as a board. They stayed in that position until the loud scream from Wanda made them pay attention to the masked man who was about to take a shot.

Tower pushed Ru aside and fired three times. All direct shots to the chest and head. The man sank down to the floor. Tower looked back. Eye Patch was motionless, his one good eye frozen, locked open in death.

When Tower looked up, Solar was running out the door and disappeared into the hallway. His footsteps echoed off the walls. Tower chased after him.

He hit the door as he approached the hallway. A check showed no sign of Solar. He ran in the direction of the sounds. Tower knew Solar had the advantage. This was his building. He would know every turn, every closet and escape route. Tower ran past the elevators. Nothing. He checked room after room, gun leading the way. Nothing.

Solar was gone.

He tried to remember the building layout.

A calm breeze and the light of a warm Florida sun greeted Brent Solar as he walked to the front door of the building. He was alone with his keyboard and a pocket full of thumb drives. Three keystrokes and the world would still be his to rule.

"Hey man. You're in my doorway." The voice came from a disheveled man who looked like he traveled some distance.

"Your doorway?," Solar was amused by the declaration from the man standing no more than six feet from him. Solar pointed to the building. "This happens to be mine. I now own this."

"You're in my doorway. I got to move you out."

"You're talking shit. Move on. I said move!"

Jervis Lanner wanted to itch his prison tats so much yet he stood there, sizing up the man who he first saw on television. The man he tracked as best he could, finally following him and waiting for the chance to see him up close.

"You're standing in my door. I need you to let me out first."

Solar was confused. "I don't know who you are but you're not making any sense. I told you to get back. I don't have time for this shit." Solar placed his hands on the keyboard. The future was in his domain.

Lanner approached a bit more. He kept his right hand behind him. The one with the eight-inch knife. The perfect knife. One Lanner picked out one night after breaking into a store. The sun glinted off the blade.

Lanner brought the knife in front of him. "I got to be right there." Lanner moved in with the speed of a bolt of lightning. The first knife stroke started across Solar's face left to right in a downward motion, swift and quiet as the inside of a forest at dawn. Solar looked stunned. His eyes bulged and he couldn't say any words.

The keyboard dropped to the ground.

The second and third slices of the knife caught Solar in the throat. A loud gurgling sound came from somewhere in Solar's body. He dropped down close to the keyboard. Then Solar was silent.

Lanner was in a groove now, his arm landing on the target several times in precise moves aimed at the defenseless Solar.

When Tower approached the front door, a long line of blood was making an overgrowing pool toward his feet. He stopped. In the doorway he saw Solar slumped over, bathed in red. There was no one else.

Tower stepped over Solar and looked around. From his left, he heard the sounds of a man running in his direction. Tower turned. Jervis was coming after him, knife in the air, his hair in disjointed locks as if flying in different directions.

Tower took aim. The first shot landed between the eyes. Jervis stopped. Tower let go two more silent hits. Both shots caught him in the chest. He went down. The knife spun around like a spin-the-bottle game. When the knife stopped, the tip was pointed at Solar.

Wanda held her hand to her mouth when she came to the front door. "What happened?" She took a step back.

"Where's Ru?"

"We caught the other guy. The second one with the mask. It helped that he fell. We were on him. We got him tied up with some wire."

Tower sighed a good sigh for the first time in days. He pulled a burner phone from his pocket. He looked around at the carnage in front of him and starting calling the cell phone for Detective Mark David.

Chapter 68

"Looks like you stopped him before he could do anything." Mark David looked over his shoulder at the large contingent of F.B.I. local Stilton Bay police, Homeland security, and a gathering crowd.

"Who is the guy with the knife?" Tower looked through the gathering for anyone he recognized.

"A guy who escaped from prison. A prison that Solar himself opened the doors."

"Weird justice," Tower said. "Hope you guys are being fair to my clients. They don't have any attorneys here."

"Don't worry. We're not filing anything. And no one has come forward to present charges in any previous situation. Once the briefing is over, they'll be free to go."

"The computers?"

The detective pointed to an unmarked van. "See that? They came in here like a bunch of drone bees. They were all over that room. And then they kicked me out. All I know is they found the thumb drives on Solar's body. They got into his computers and they're dismantling everything he set up. Then they've got to study how he did it. Maybe we can all learn something from this one."

"Maybe." Tower turned the silence over to Mark David. "Let's trade. I'll take my Glock back."

"It's part of the investigation. It might be awhile."

"No problem."

"How did you know about this room." David's face was laced with bent brow lines.

Tower drew a deep breath. "Solar has always made this personal. I mean, he blew up his boss. Like the thumb-drives, he took plenty of time to plan things. I figured he would need a serve room. And what better place than his own building. I dug up the plans and they had that room with no designation. I just thought that was it."

"Nice find."

"Who was this guy, Eye Patch?"

Detective David scratched at his chin as if deciding what was classified and what he could tell Tower. "He was a mid-level buyer of just about everything. Three years ago, he headed a group selling stolen online ID's. The group also stole thousands of credit card numbers. Then he went solo and tried to work out a deal with Brent Solar. We think his plan was to start in the Middle East and keep going until he found a buyer for all the hacked information."

"Until Solar changed the plans."

"He has several names. Stuff I can't talk about yet." David started walking toward the other end of the parking lot. "Glad you're okay. And by the way, all that money in your account?"

"I know," Tower said, "It's part of the investigation."

Both men smiled.

Ru and Wanda emerged from a different van and approached Tower. "They asked me more questions than my fifth grade science teacher," Ru said. "I didn't like it then and I don't like it now."

"At least we can get out of here," Wanda pulled on her more than tight jeans. "They say we're all entitled to a reward that was posted on Solar."

"You two take it," Tower told them.

"But we were all part of this." Wanda extended her hand.

"It's okay. You two take it."

Ru stared at him. "Sweetheart, that's a lot of money." She lowered her words so only Tower could hear. "We can get out of the hunting business."

"So what will you two do? They say you are free to go. Just remember, you two have a clean slate."

They looked at each other, then Wanda answered him. "Maybe we'll go private."

"Like private detective," Ru said.

"Whatever you do, you have my number. Good luck to you."

They walked away, in Ru and Wanda style, slow.

"You want to go after them?" Shannon stepped in front of Tower so that his attention had to be focused only on her. "They tell me you can leave this place."

"What do you want to do?" Tower asked.

"Well, you need to see Jackie. And after that, maybe I can help you rest up."

Tower and Shannon stood under the outstretched branches of a ficus tree. Shannon's eyes remained bright even in the dappled light. For a moment only the chirp of a blue jay pierced the air. "I'd like to tell you all about it."

Tower pushed his hand into hers, waiting to see if she would draw back or take his invitation. She held his hand.

Shannon smiled at him. “I kept telling myself I should trust you.”

Tower said, “Thank you. I’ll tell you everything that happened over dinner.”

AUTHOR'S NOTE:

Stilton Bay is the author's creation and is not a real city in Florida. Hopefully my creation is as beautiful as the cities in the state.